HEIR TO EMPIRE

Var was the second man Sos had ever called a friend. Sos trained him with the sticks until there was no one mightier in the circle.

Var was the chosen, destined to reign, until he slew Sos' most secret and dearly held love. The passion of his pursuit would only be matched by the wrath of his revenge.

VAR THE STICK
by Piers Anthony

Also by PIERS ANTHONY

Sos the Rope*
Neq the Sword†

*published by Corgi Books
†to be published by Corgi Books

Var the Stick

Piers Anthony

CORGI BOOKS
A DIVISION OF TRANSWORLD PUBLISHERS LTD

VAR THE STICK
A CORGI BOOK 0 552 09736 5

First publication in Great Britain 1975

PRINTING HISTORY
Corgi edition published 1975

Corgi Books are published by
Transworld Publishers Ltd.,
Cavendish House, 57–59 Uxbridge Road,
Ealing, London W.5.
Made and printed in the United States of America
by Arcata Graphics,
Buffalo, New York

CHAPTER 1

Tyl of Two Weapons waited in the night cornfield. He had one singlestick in his hand and the other tucked in his waist band, ready to draw. He had waited two hours in silence.

Tyl was a handsome man, sleek but muscular. His face was set in a habitual frown stemming from years of less than ideal command. The empire spanned a thousand miles, and he was second only to the Master in its hierarchy, and first in most practical matters. He set interim policy within the general guidelines laid down by the Master, and established the rankings and placement of the major subchiefs. Tyl had power—but it chafed at him.

Then he heard it: a rustle to the north that was not typical of the local animals.

Carefully he stood, shielded from the intruder by the tall plants. There was no moon, for the beast never came in the light. Tyl traced its progress toward the fence by the subtle sounds. The wind was from the north; otherwise the thing would have caught his scent and stayed clear.

There was no doubt about it. This was his quarry. Now it was mounting the sturdy split-rail fence, scrambling over, landing with a faint thump within the corn. And now it was quiet for a time, waiting to see whether it had been discovered. A cunning animal—one that avoided deadfalls, ignored poison and fought savagely when trapped. In the past month three of Tyl's men had been wounded in night encounters with this creature. Already it was becoming known as a hex upon the camp, an omen of ill, and skilled warriors were evincing an unseemly fear of the dark.

And so it was up to the chief to resolve the matter. Tyl, long bored by the routine of maintaining a tribe that was

1

not engaged in conquest, was more than satisfied by the challenge. He had no awe of the supernatural. He intended to capture the thing and display it before the tribe: Here is the spook that made cowards of lesser men!

Capture, not death, for this quarry. This was the reason he had brought his sticks instead of his sword.

Slight noise again. Now it was foraging, stripping the ripening corn from the stalk and consuming it on the spot. This alone set it apart from ordinary carnivores, for they would never have touched the corn. But it could not be an ordinary herbivore either, for they did not harvest and chew the cobs like that. And its footprints, visible in daylight following a raid, were not those of any animal he knew. Broad and round, with the marks of four squat claws or slender hoofs —not a bear, not anything natural.

It was time. Tyl advanced on the creature, holding one stick aloft, using his free hand to part the cornstalks quietly. He knew he could not come upon it completely by surprise, but he hoped to get close enough to take it with a sudden charge. Tyl knew himself to be the best fighter in the world, with the sticks. The only man who could beat him, stick to stick, was dead, gone to the mountain. There was nothing Tyl feared when so armed.

He recalled that lone defeat with nostalgia, as he made the tedious approach. It was four years ago, when he had been young. Sol had done it—Sol of All Weapons, creator of the empire—the finest warrior of all time. Sol had set out to conquer the world, with Tyl as his chief lieutenant. And they had been doing it, too—until the Nameless One had come.

He was close now, and abruptly the foraging noises ceased. The thing had heard him!

Tyl did not wait for the animal to make up its crafty mind. He launched himself at it, heedless of the shocks of corn he damaged in his mad passage. Now he had both sticks ready, batting stalks aside as he ran.

The creature bolted. Tyl saw a hairy hump rise in the darkness, heard its weird grunt. He was tempted to use his flash but knew it would destroy the night vision he had built up in the silent wait and put his mission in peril. The animal was at the fence now, but the fence was strong and high, and Tyl knew he could catch it before it got over.

The creature knew it too. Its back to the course rails, it came to bay, it's breath rasping. Tyl saw the dim glint of its eye, the vague outline of its body, shaggy and warped and menacing. Tyl laid into it with both sticks, seeking a quick head blow that would reduce it to impotence.

But the thing was as canny about weapons as about traps. It dived, passing under his defense in the obscurity, and fastened its teeth on Tyl's knee. He clubbed it on the head once, twice, feeling the give of the tangled fur, and it let go. The wound was not serious, as the thing's snout was recessed and its teeth blunt, but Tyl's knees had been tricky since the Nameless One had smashed them a year before. And he was angry at his defensive negligence; nothing should have penetrated his guard like that, by day or night.

It drew back, snarling, and Tyl was chilled by that sound. No wolf, no wildcat, articulated like that. And now, as it tasted blood, its mewling became hungry as well as defiant.

It pounced, not smoothly but with force. This time it went for his throat, as he had known it would. He rapped its head again with the stick, but again it anticipated him, hunching so that the blow skidded glancingly off the skull. It struck Tyl's chest, bearing him down, and its foreclaws raked his neck while its hindclaws dug for his groin.

Tyl, dismayed by its ferocity, beat it off blindly, and it jumped away. Before he could recover it was up again, scrambling over the fence while he hobbled behind, too late.

Now he cursed aloud in fury at its escape, but the expletives were tinged with a certain brute respect. He had chosen the locale of combat, and the marauder had bested him in this context. He would have to revile it, but there was a use he could make of this situation, perhaps a better one than he had had in mind before.

The creature dropped outside the fence and loped off into the forest. It was bleeding from a wound reopened by the blows of the attacker, and it was partially lame on flat ground because of malformed bones in its feet. But it made rapid progress, its armored toes finding good purchase in the wilder turf.

And it was clever. It had seen Tyl clearly and smelled him. Only its pressing hunger had dulled its alertness prior to the encounter. It had recognized the singlesticks as weapons and had avoided them. Still, blows had landed, and they had hurt. The creature thought about it, turning the problem over in its mind as it angled toward the badlands. The menfolk were getting more difficult about their crops. Now they lay in wait, ambushed, attacked, pursued. This last had been quite effective; if the hunger were not so strong, the area would be best avoided entirely. As it was, better protection would have to be devised.

It entered the badlands where no man could follow and slowed to catch its breath. It picked up a branch, curling stubby mottled digits around it tightly. The forelimb was angular, the claws wide and flat—less effective as a weapon than as supplementary protection for the tips of the calloused fingers. It wrestled the stick around, finding comfortable purchase, imitating the stance of the man in the cornfield. It banged the wood against a tree, liking the feel of the impact. It banged harder, and the dry, rotted branch shattered, releasing a stunned grub. The creature quickly pounced on this, squishing it dead and licking the squirting juices with gusto, forgetting the useless stick. But it had learned something.

Next time it foraged it would take along a stick.

CHAPTER 2

The Master of Empire pondered the message from Tyl of Two Weapons. Tyl had not written the note himself, of course, for like most of the nomadic leaders he was illiterate. But his smart wife, Tyla, like many of the empire women, had taken up the art with enthusiasm, and was now a fair hand at the written language.

The Master was literate, and he believed in literacy, yet he had not encouraged the women's classes in reading and figuring. The Master knew the advantages of farming, too, yet he ignored the farms. And he comprehended the dynamics of empire, for he, in other guise, had fashioned this same empire and brought it from formless ambition to a mighty force. Yet he now let it drift and stagnate and atrophy.

Tyl's message was deferentially worded, but it constituted a clever challenge to his authority and policy. Tyl was an activist, impatient to resume conquest. He wanted either to goose the Master into action or to ease him out of power so that new leadership might bring a new policy. Because Tyl himself was bonded to this regime, he could do nothing directly. He would not go against the man who had bested him in the circle. This was not cowardice but honor.

If the Master declined to deal with this mysterious menace to the local crops, he would be admitting either timidity or treason to the purpose of the empire. For farming was vital to growth; the organized nomads could not afford to remain dependent on the largesse of the crazies. If he did not support the farm program the resultant unrest would throw him into disrepute and lead to solidification of resistance around some other figure. He could not afford that, for he would then soon be spending all his time defeating such weedlike pretenders in the circle. No—he had to rule the empire and keep it quiescent.

So there was nothing to do but tackle this artfully posed problem. He could be sure it was not an easy one, for this wild beast had wounded Tyl himself and escaped. That suggested that no lesser man than the Master could subdue it.

Of course he could organize a large hunting party, but this would violate the precepts of single combat, and it went against the grain, even when an animal was involved. In fact, it would be another implication of cowardice.

It was necessary that the Master prove himself against this beast. That was what Tyl wanted, for failure would certainly damage his image. He did not appreciate being maneuvered, but the alternatives were worse, and he did privately admire the manner in which Tyl had set this up. The man would be a valuable ally at such time as certain things changed.

So it was the Nameless One, the Man of No Weapon, Master of Empire, this leader took leave of the wife he had usurped from the former master, put routine affairs in the hands of competent subordinates and set out on foot alone for Tyl's encampment. He wore a cloak over his grotesque and mighty body, but all who saw him in that region knew him and feared him. His hair was white, his visage ugly, and there was no man to match him in the circle.

In fifteen days he arrived. A young staffer who had never seen the Master challenged him at the border of the camp. The Nameless One took that staff and tied a knot in it and handed it back. "Show this to Tyl of Two Weapons," he said.

And Tyl came hurriedly with his entourage. He ordered the guard with the pretzel staff to the fields to work among the women, as penalty for not recognizing the visitor. But the Weaponless said, "He was right to challenge when in doubt; let the man who straightens that weapon chastise him, no other." So he was not punished, for no one except a smithy could have unbent that metal rod. And no other man of that camp failed to know the Nameless One by sight thereafter.

Next morning the Master took up a bow and a length of rope, for these were not weapons of the circle, and set off on the trail of the raider. He took along a hound and a pack of supplies doubly loaded, but would tolerate the company of no other man. "I will bring the creature back," he said.

Tyl made no comment, thinking his own thoughts.

The trail passed from the open fields of corn and buckwheat to the birches fringing the forestland, and on toward the dwindling region of local badland. The Master observed the markers that the crazies placed and periodically resurveyed. Unlike the average person, he had no superstitions, no fear of these. He knew that it was radiation that made these areas deadly—roentgen left from the fabled Blast. Every year there was less of it, and the country at the fringe of the badlands became habitable for plant, animal and man. He knew that so long as the native life was healthy, there was little danger from radiation.

But there were other terrors in the fringe. Tiny shrews swarmed periodically, consuming all animals in their path and devouring each other when nothing else was available. Large white moths came out at night, their stings deadly. And there were wild tales told by firelight of strange haunted buildings, armored bones and living machines. The Master did not credit much of this and sought some reasonable explanation for what he did credit. But he did know the badlands were dangerous, and he entered them with caution.

The traces skirted the heart of the radioactive area, staying a mile or so within the crazy boundary. This told the Master something else important: that the creature he hunted was not some supernatural spook from the deep horror region, but an animal of the fringe, leery of radiation. That meant he could run it down in time.

For two days he followed the trail the cheerful hound sniffed out. He fed the dog and himself from his pack, occasionally bringing down a rabbit with an arrow and cooking it whole as a mutual treat. He slept on the open ground, well covered. This was late summer, and the warm crazy sleeping bag sufficed. He had a spare, in case. He rather enjoyed the trek and did not push the pace.

On the evening of the second day he found it. The hound bayed and raced ahead, then yelped and ran back frightened.

The thing stood under a large oak: It was about four feet tall, bipedal, hunched. Wild hair radiated from its head and curled about its muzzle. Mats of shaggy fur hung over its shoulders. Its skin, where it showed on head and limbs and torso, was mottled gray and yellow and encrusted with dirt.

But it was no animal. It was a mutant human boy.

The boy had made a crude club. He made as though to

attack his pursuer, having naturally been aware of the Master for some time. But the sheer size of the man daunted him, and he fled, running on the balls of his blunted, calloused feet.

The Nameless One made camp there. He had suspected that the raider was human or human-derived, for no animal had the degree of cunning and dexterity this prowler had shown. But now that he had made the confirmation, he needed to reconsider means. It would not do to kill this boy, yet it would hardly be kind to bring him back prisoner for the torment the angry farmer-warriors would inflict. Civilization grew very thin in such a case. But one or the other had to be accomplished, for the Master had his own political expedience to consider.

He thought it out, slowly, powerfully. He decided to take the boy to his own camp so that the lad could join human society without compelling prejudice. This would mean months, perhaps years, of demanding attention.

The white moths were coming out. He covered his head with netting, sealed his bag and settled down for sleep. He knew of no reliable way to protect the dog, for the animal would not comprehend the necessity for confinement in the spare bag. He hoped the animal would not snap at a moth and get stung. He wondered how the boy survived in this region. He thought about Sola, the woman he once had loved, the wife he now pretended to love. He thought of Sol, the friend he had sent to the mountain, the man for whom he would trade all his empire just to travel together again and converse without trial of strength. And he thought lingeringly of the woman of Helicon, his true wife, and the woman he really loved but would never see again. Great thoughts, petty thoughts. He suffered. He slept.

Next morning the chase resumed. The dog was well; it seemed that the moths did not attack wantonly. Perhaps they died when delivered of their toxin, in the manner of bees. Probably a man could expose himself safely if he only treated them deferentially. That might explain the boy's survival.

The trail led deeper into the badlands. Now they would discover who had more courage and determination: pursuer or fugitive.

The boy had obviously haunted this area for some time. If there were lethal radiation he should have died already. In any event, the Master could probably withstand any dosage the boy could. So if the lad hoped to escape by hiding in the hot region, he would be disappointed.

Still, the Master could not entirely repress his apprehension as the trail led into a landscape of stunted and deformed trees. Surely these had been touched. And game was scarce, tokening the irregular ravages of the fringe-shrews. If radiation were not present now, it had not departed long since.

He caught up to the boy again. The hunched condition of the youngster's body was more evident by full daylight, his piebald skin more striking. And the way he ran—heels high, knees bent so that the whole foot never touched the ground, forelimbs dropping down periodically for support—this was uncanny. Had this boy ever shared a human home?

"Come!" the Weaponless called. "Yield to me and I will spare your life and give you food."

But as he had expected, the fugitive paid no attention. Probably this wilderness denizen had never learned to speak.

The trees became mere shrubs, scabbed with discolored wood-rinds and sap-bleeding abrasions, and their leaves were limp, sticky, asymmetric efforts. Then only shriveled sticks protruded from the burned soil, twisted grotesquely. Finally all life was gone, leaving caked ashes and greenish glass. The hound whined, afraid of the dead bare terrain, and the Master felt rather like whining himself, for this was grim.

But still the boy ran ahead, bounding circuitously around invisible obstacles. At first the Nameless One thought it was strategy, to confuse the pursuit. Then, as he perceived the maneuvering to take forms that were by no means evasive or concealing, he pondered dementia. Radiation might indeed make a victim mad before it destroyed. Finally he realized that the boy was actually skirting pockets of radiation. *He could tell where the roentgen remained!*

Dangerous terrain indeed! The Nameless One followed the trail exactly and kept the hound to it, knowing that shortcuts would expose him to invisible misery. He was risking his health and his life, but he would not relent.

"Are you ashamed because you are ugly?" he called. He took off his great cloak and showed his own massive, scarred torso, and his neck so laced with gristle that it resembled the trunk of an aged yellow birch. "You are not more ugly than I!"

But the boy ran on.

Then the Master paused, for ahead he saw a building.

Buildings were scarce in the nomad culture. There were
hostels that the crazies maintained, where wandering warriors and their families might stay for a night or a fortnight
without obligation except to take due care with the premises.
There were the houses of the crazies themselves and the
school buildings and offices they maintained. And of course
there were the subterranean fortifications of the underworld,
wherein were manufactured the weapons and clothing the
nomads used, though only the crazies and the Master himself
knew this. But the great expanse of land was field and fern
and forest, cleared by the Blast that had destroyed the marvelous warlike culture of the Ancients. The wilderness had
returned in the wake of the radiation, open and clean.

This building was tremendous and misshapen. The Master
counted seven distinct levels within it, one layered atop another, and above the last fiber-clothed story metal rods projected like the ribs of a dead cow. Behind it was another
structure of similar configuration and beyond that a third.

He contemplated these, amazed. He had read about such
a thing in the old books, but had half believed it was a myth.
This was a "city."

Before the Blast, the texts had claimed, mankind had
grown phenomenally numerous and strong and had resided in
cities where every conceivable (and inconceivable) comfort of
life was available. Then these fabulously prosperous peoples
had destroyed it all in a rain of fire, a smash of intolerable
radiation, leaving only the scattered nomads and crazies and
underworlders, and the extensive badlands.

He could poke a thousand logical holes in that fable. For
one thing, it was obvious that no culture approaching the
technological level described would be at the same time so
primitive as to throw it away so pointlessly. And such a
radically different culture as that of the nomads could not
have sprung full-blown from ashes. But he was sure the ultimate truth did lie hidden somewhere within the badlands, for
their very presence seemed to vindicate the reality of the
Blast, whatever its true cause.

Now, astonishingly, these badlands were ready to yield
some of their secrets. For the century since the cataclysm no
man had penetrated far into the posted regions and lived.
But always the proscribed area declined. He knew the time
would come, though not in his lifetime, when the entire
territory would be open once more to man. Meanwhile the

fever of discovery was on him; he was so eager to learn the truth that he gladly risked the roentgen.

The boy's tracks were clear in the dirt that had been freshened by recent rainfall. The glass had broken up and disappeared here; sprouts of pale grass rimmed the path. Nothing, not even the radiation, was consistent about the badlands.

The boy had gone into the building. Most nomads were in awe of solid structures of any size and avoided even the comparatively modest buildings of the crazies. But the Master had traveled widely and experienced as much as any man of his time, and he knew that there was nothing supernatural about a giant edifice. There could be danger, yes, but the natural hazards of falling timbers and deep pits and radiation and crazed animals, nothing more sinister.

Still he hesitated before entering that ancient temple. It would be easy to become trapped inside, and perhaps the wily boy had something of that sort in mind. He had been known to place deadfalls for unwary trackers, laboriously scraped out of the earth by hand and nail and artfully covered. That was one of the things he had evidently learned from the measures applied against *him*. Too smart for an animal—adding to the terror surrounding him—and not bad for a human.

The Master looked about. Within the shelter of the window arches there were fragments of dry wood. Most had rotted, but not all. There was bound to be more wood inside. He could fire it and drive the boy out. This seemed to be the safest course.

Yet there could be valuable artifacts within, machines, books, supplies. Was he to destroy it all so wantonly? Better to preserve the building intact and assemble a task force to explore it thoroughly at a later date.

So deciding, the Master entered at the widest portal and began his final search for the boy. The hound whined and stayed so close that it was tricky to avoiding tripping over it; but the animal did sniff out the trail.

There were stone steps leading down, an avenue of splendid and wasteful breadth, and this was where the boy had gone. And, so easily that it was suspicious, they had tracked the marauder to his lair. There did not seem to be another exit apart from the stair. The boy had to be waiting below.

Would it be wise to check the upper floors first? The boy

might actually be leading him into the final trap, while his real residence was above. No, best to follow closely, for otherwise he ran too strong a risk of encountering radiation. Had he realized that the chase would end so deep in the badlands he would have arranged to obtain a crazy geiger. As it was, he had to proceed with extreme caution. That meant, in this case, to dispense with much of his caution in the pursuit. Physical attack by the boy was much less to be feared than the radiation that might be lurking on either side of the boy's trail.

As the Nameless One approached the final chamber, an object flew out. The boy, unable to flee again, was pelting his tormentor with any objects available.

The Master paused, contemplating the thing that had been thrown. He squatted to pick it up, watching the door so that he would not be taken by surprise. Then he turned the object over in his hands, studying it closely.

It was metal, but not a can or tool. A weapon, but no sword or staff or dagger. One end was solid and curved around at right angles to the rest; the other end was hollow. The thing had a good solid heft to it, and there were assorted minor mechanisms attached.

The Master's hands shook as he recognized it. This too had been described in the books; this too was an artifact of the old times.

It was a gun.

CHAPTER 3

The boy stood astride the boxes and made ready to throw another metal rock, for the tremendous man and the tame animal had trapped him here. Never before had pursuit been so relentless; never before had he had to defend his lair. Had he anticipated this, he would have hidden elsewhere.

But there were so many places here that burned his skin and drove him back! This building was the only one completely safe.

The giant appeared again in the doorway. The boy threw his rock and reached for another. But this time the man jerked aside, letting the missile glance off his bulging thigh, and heaved a length of rope forward. The boy found himself entangled and, in a moment, helpless. It was as though that rope were alive, the way it twisted and coiled and jerked.

The man bound him and slung him over one tremendous shoulder and carried him out of the room and up the stairs and from the building. The man's brute strength was appalling. The boy tried to squirm and bite, but his teeth met flesh like baked leather.

His skin burned as the man passed through a hot region. Was the monster invulnerable to this too? He had charged through several similar areas on the way in, areas the boy had meticulously avoided. How could one fight such a force?

In the forest the man set him down and loosed the rope, making man sounds that were only dimly familiar. The boy bolted as soon as he was free.

The rope sailed out like a striking snake and wrapped itself about his waist hauling him back. He was captive again. "No," the man said, and that sound was a clear negation.

The giant removed the rope again, and immediately the boy dashed away. Once more he was lassoed.

"No!" the man repeated, and this time his huge hand came across in a blow that seemed nearly to cave in the boy's chest. The boy fell to the ground, conscious of nothing but his pain and the need for air.

A third time the man unwound the rope. This time the boy remained where he was. Lessons of this nature were readily learned.

They walked on toward the main camp, still far distant. The boy led, for the eyes of the man never left him. The boy avoided the diminishing patches of radiation, and man and animal followed. By evening they had come to the place they had seen each other the previous day.

The man opened his pack and brought out chunks of material that smelled good. He bit off some, chewing with gusto, and passed some along to the boy. The invitation did not have to be repeated, for this was food.

After eating, the man urinated against a tree and covered his body again. The boy followed the example, even imitating the upright stance. He had learned long ago to control his eliminations, for carelessly deposited traces could interfere with hunting, but it had never occurred to him to direct the flow with his hand.

"Here," the man said. He threw the boy down gently and shoved him feet-first into a constraining sack. The boy struggled as some kind of mesh covered his head. "Stay there tonight, or—" And the ponderous fist came down, to tap only lightly at the bruised chest. Another warning.

Then the man went apart a certain distance and climbed into another bag, and the dog settled down under the tree.

The boy lay there, needing to escape but hesitant to brace the dangers of the night this close to the hot region. He could see well enough and usually foraged in the dark, but not *here*. He had been stung once by a white moth and had nearly perished. It was possible to avoid them, but never with certainty, for they rested under leaves and sometimes on the ground. Here beneath the netting he was at least protected.

But if he did not flee by night, he would not have the chance by day. The rope was too swift and clever, the giant too strong.

He could see that the man was sleeping and decided. He sat up and began to claw his way out.

The man woke at the first sound. "No!" he called.

It was hazardous to defy the giant, who might run him down again anyway. The boy lay back, resigned. And slept.

In the morning they ate again. It had been a long time since the boy had had two such easy meals in succession. It was a condition he could learn to like.

The man then conveyed him to a stream and washed them both. He applied ointments from his pack to the assorted bruises and scratches on the boy's body and replaced the uncured animal skins with an oversize shirt and pantaloons. After this disgusting process they resumed the journey toward the mancamp.

The boy shrugged and chafed under the awful clothing. He thought once more of bolting for freedom before being taken entirely out of his home territory, but a grunted warning changed his mind. And the fact was that the man, apart from his pecularities of dress and urination, was not a harsh captor. He did not punish without provocation and even showed gruff kindness.

About the middle of the day the man's pace slowed. He seemed weary or sleepy, despite his enormous muscles and stamina. He began to stagger. He stopped and disgorged his breakfast, and the boy wondered whether this was another civilized ritual. Then he sat down on the ground and looked unhappy.

The boy watched for a time. When the man did not rise, the boy began to walk away. Unchallenged, he ran swiftly back the way they had come. He was free!

About a mile away he stopped and threw off the fettering man-clothing. Then he paused. He knew what was wrong with the giant. The man was not immune to the hot places; he simply hadn't been aware of them, so had exposed himself recklessly. Now he was coming down with the sickness.

The boy had learned about this, too, the hard way. He had been burned and had become weak and vomited and felt like dying. But he had survived, and after that his skin had been sensitized, and whenever he approached a hot area he felt the burn immediately. His brothers, lacking the skin patches that set him apart, had had no such ability and had died gruesomely. He had also discovered certain leaves that cooled his skin somewhat, and the juices of certain fringe-plant stems eased his stomach of such sickness. But he never ventured voluntarily into the hot sections. His skin always warned him off in time, and he took the other medicines purely as a precautionary procedure.

The giant man would be very sick, and probably he would die. At night the moths would come, and later the shrews, while he lay helpless. The man had been stupid to enter the badlands' heart.

Stupid—yet brave and kind. No other stranger had ever extended a helping hand to the boy or fed him since his parents died, and he was oddly moved by it. Somewhere deep in his memory he found a basic instruction: kindness must be met with kindness. It was all that remained of the teaching of his long-lost parents, whose skulls were whitening in a burn.

This giant man was like his dead father: strong, quiet, fierce in anger but gentle when unprovoked. The boy had appreciated both the attention and the savage discipline. It was possible to trust a man like that.

He gathered select herbs and came back, his motives uncertain but his actions sure. The man was lying where he had originally settled to the ground, his body flushed. The boy placed a compress of leaves against the fever-ridden torso and limbs and squeezed drops of stem-juice into the grimacing mouth, he could do little else. The giant was too heavy for him to move, and the boy's clubbed hands could not grasp him properly for such an effort. Not without bruising the flesh.

But as the coolness of night came, the man revived somewhat. He cleaned himself up with agonized motions but did not eat. He climbed into his bag and lost consciousness.

In the morning the man seemed alert but stumbled when he attempted to stand. He could not walk. The boy gave him a stem to chew on, and he chewed, not seeming to be aware of his action.

The food in the pack ran out on the following day, and the boy went foraging. Certain fruits were ripening, certain wild tubers swelling. He plucked and dug these, bound them in the jacket he no longer wore and loped with the bundle back to their enforced camp. In this manner he sustained them both.

On the fourth day the man began bleeding from the skin. Some parts of his body were as hard as wood and did not bleed; but where the skin was natural, it hemorrhaged. The man touched himself with dismay but could not hold on to consciousness.

The boy took cloth from the pack and soaked it in water and bathed the blood away. But when more blood came, appearing as if magically on the surface though there was no abrasion, he let it collect and cake. This slowed the flow. He knew that blood had to be kept inside the body, for he had bled copiously once when wounded and had felt very weak for many days. And when animals bled too much, they died.

Whenever the man revived, the boy gave him fruit and the special stems to eat, and whatever water he could accept without choking. When he sank again into stupor, the boy packed the moist leaves tightly about him. When it grew cold, he covered the man with the bag he slept in, and lay beside him, shielding him from the worst of the night wind.

The dog crawled away and died.

Days passed. The sick man burned up his own flesh, becoming gaunt, and the contours of his body were bizarre. It was as though he wore stones and boards under the skin, so that no point could penetrate; but with the supportive flesh melting away, the armor hung loosely. It hampered his breathing, his elimination. But perhaps it had also stopped some of the radiation, for the boy knew that physical substance could do this to a certain extent.

The man was near death, but he refused to die. The boy watched, aware that he was spectator to a greater courage battling a more horrible antagonist than any man could hope to conquer. The boy's own father and brothers had yielded up their lives far more readily. Blood and sweat and urine matted the leaves, and dirt and debris covered the man, but still he fought.

And finally he began to mend. His fever passed, the bleeding stopped, some of his strength returned and he ate—at first tentatively, then with huge appetite. He looked at the boy with renewed comprehension, and he smiled.

There was a bond between them now. Man and boy were friends.

CHAPTER 4

The warriors gathered around the central circle. Tyl of Two Weapons supervised the ceremony. "Who is there would claim the honor of manhood and take a name this day?" he inquired somewhat perfunctorily. He had been doing this every month for eight years, and it bored him.

Several youths stepped up: gangling adolescents who seemed hardly to know how to hang on to their weapons. Every year the crop seemed younger and gawkier. Tyl longed for the old days, when he had first served Sol of All Weapons. Then men had been men, and the leader had been a leader, and great things had been in the making. Now—weaklings and inertia.

It was no effort to put the ritual scorn into his voice. "You will fight each other," he told them. "I will pair you off, man to man in the circle. He who retains the circle shall be deemed warrior and be entitled to name and band and weapon with honor. The other. . . ."

He did not bother to finish. No one could be called a warrior unless he won at least once in the circle. Some hopefuls failed again and again, and some eventually gave up and went to the crazies or the mountain. Most went to other tribes and tried again.

"You, club," Tyl said, picking out a chubby would-be clubber. "You, staff," selecting an angular hopeful staffer.

The two youths, visibly nervous, stepped gingerly into the circle. They began to fight, the clubber making huge clumsy swings, the staffer countering ineptly. By and by the club smashed one of the staffer's misplaced hands, and the staff fell to the ground.

That was enough for the staffer. He bounced out of the

circle. It made Tyl sick, not for the fact of victory and defeat, but for the sheer incompetence of it. How could such dolts ever become proper warriors? What good would a winner such as this clubber be for the tribe, whose decisive blow had been sheer fortune?

But it was never possible to be certain, he reflected. Some of the very poorest prospects that he sent along to Sav the Staff's training camp emerged as formidable warriors. The real mark of a man was how he responded to training. That had been the lesson that earlier weaponless man had taught, the one that never fought in the circle. What was his name? Sos. Sos had stayed with the tribe a year and established the system, then departed forever. Except for some brief thing about a rope. Not much of a man, but a good mind. Yes, it was best to incorporate the clubber into the tribe and send him to Sav; good might even come of it. If not, no loss.

Next were a pair of daggers. This fight was bloody, but at least the victor looked like a potential man.

Then a sworder took on a sticker. Tyl watched this contest with interest, for his own two weapons were sword and sticks, and he wished he had more of each in his tribe. The sticks were useful for discipline, the sword for conquest.

The sticker-novice seemed to have some promise. His hands were swift, his aim sure. The sworder was strong but slow; he laid about himself crudely.

The sticker caught his opponent on the side of the head and followed up the telling blow with a series to the neck and shoulders. So doing, he let slip his guard, and the keen blade edge caught him at the throat, and he was dead.

Tyl closed his eyes in pain. Such folly! The one youngster with token promise had let his enthusiasm run away with him and had walked into a slash that any idiot could have avoided. Was there any hope for this generation?

One youth remained—a rare morningstar. It took courage to select such a weapon, and a certain morbidity, for it was devastating and unstable. Tyl had left him until last because he wanted to match him against an experienced warrior. That would greatly decrease the star's chance of success, but would correspondingly increase his chance of survival. If he looked good, Tyl would arrange to match him next month with an easy mark and take him into the tribe as soon as he had his band and name.

One of the perimeter sentries came up. "Strangers, Chief—man and woman. He's ugly as hell; she must be too."

Still irritated by the loss of the promising sticker, Tyl snapped back: "Is your bracelet so worn you can't tell an ugly woman by sight?"

"She's veiled."

Tyl became interested. "What woman would cover her face?"

The sentry shrugged. "Do you want me to bring them here?"

Tyl nodded.

As the man departed, he returned to the problem of the star. A veteran staffer would be best, for the morningstar could maim or kill the wielders of other weapons, even in the hands of a novice. He summoned a man who had had experience with the star in the circle and began giving him instructions.

Before the test commenced, the strangers arrived. The man was indeed ugly: somewhat hunchbacked, with hands grossly gnarled and large patches of discolored skin on limbs and torso. Because of his stoop, his eyes peered out from below shaggy brows, oddly impressive. He moved gracefully despite some peculiarity of gait; there was something wrong with his feet. His aspect was feral.

The woman was shrouded in a long cloak that concealed her figure as the veil concealed her face. But he could tell from the way she stepped that she was neither young nor fat. That, unless she gave him some pretext to have her stripped, was as much as he was likely to know.

"I am Tyl, chief of this camp in the name of the Nameless One," he said to the man. "What is your business here?"

The man displayed his left wrist. It was naked.

"You came to earn a bracelet?" Tyl was surprised that a man as muscular and scarred and altogether formidable as this one should not already be a warrior. But another look at the almost useless hands seemed to clarify that. How could he fight well, unless he could grasp his weapon?

Or could he be another weaponless warrior? Tyl knew of only one in the empire, but that one was *the* Weaponless, the Master. It could indeed be done; Tyl himself had gone down to defeat in the circle before that juggernaut.

"What is your chosen weapon?" he asked.

The man reached to his belt and revealed, hanging beneath the loose folds of his jacket, a pair of singlesticks.

Tyl was both relieved and disappointed. A novice weaponless warrior would have been intriguing. Then he had another notion. "Will you go against the star?"

The man, still not speaking, nodded.

Tyl gestured to the circle. "Star, here is your match," he called.

The size of the audience seemed to double as he spoke. This contest promised to be interesting!

The star stepped into the circle, hefting his spiked ball. The stranger removed his jacket and leggings to stand in conventional pantaloons that still looked odd on him. His chest, though turned under by his posture, was massive. Across it the flesh was yellowish. The legs were extremely stout, ridged with muscle, and the short feet were bare. The toenails curled around the toes thickly, almost like hoofs. Strange man!

The arms were not proportionately developed, though on a man with lighter chest and shoulders they would have been impressive enough. But the hands, as they closed about the sticks, resembled pincers. The grip was square, unsophisticated, awkward—but tight. This novice was either very bad or very good.

The veiled woman settled near the circle to watch. She was as strange in her concealment as the young hunchback was in his physique.

The sticker entered the circle circumspectly, like an animal skirting a deadfall, but his guard was up. The star whirled his chained mace above his head so that the spokes whistled in the air. For a moment the two faced each other at the ready. Then the star advanced, the wheel of his revolving sledge coming to intersect the body of his opponent.

The sticker ducked, as he had to; no flesh could withstand the strike of that armored ball. His powerful legs carried him along bent over, and his natural hunch facilitated this; half his normal height, he raced across the circle and came up behind the star.

That one ploy told half the story. Tyl knew that if the sticker could jump as well as he could stoop, the star would never catch him. And the star had to catch him soon, for the whirling ball was quickly fatiguing to the elevated arm.

But it never came to that. Before the star could reorient, the sticks had clipped him about the business arm, and he was unable to maintain his pose. The motion of the ball slowed; the man staggered.

Seeing that he was too stupid to realize he had already lost and to step out of the circle, Tyl spoke for the man: "Star yields."

The star looked about, confused. "But I'm still in the circle!"

Tyl had no patience with folly. "Stay, then."

The man started to wheel his ball again, unsteadily. The sticker stepped close and rapped him on the skull. As man and ball fell, the sticker put one of his sticks between his own teeth and used the free hand to clamp onto the chain. This was an interesting maneuver, because the typical star chain was spiked with tiny, needle-pointed barbs against just such contact. But the sticker seemed not to notice. He dragged the unconscious man to the edge of the ring, then let go and bent to roll him out.

With something akin to genuine pleasure, Tyl presented the grotesque sticker with the golden band of manhood. He noticed that the man's hands were enormously callused. No wonder he did not fear barbs! "Henceforth, warrior, be called—" Tyl paused. "What name have you chosen?"

The man tried to speak, but his voice was rasping. It was as though he had calluses on his larynx, too. The word that came out sounded like a growl.

Tyl took it in stride. "Henceforth be called Var—Var the Stick." Then: "Who is your companion?"

Var shook his shaggy leaning head, not answering. But the woman came forth of her own accord, removing her veil and cloak.

"Sola!" Tyl exclaimed, recognizing the wife of the Master. She was still a handsome woman, though it had been almost ten years since he had first seen her. She had stayed about four years with Sol, then gone to the new Master of Empire. Because the conqueror was weaponless and wore no bracelet and used no name, she had kept the band and name she had. This was tantamount to adultery, openly advertised, but the Master had won her fairly. He was the mightiest man ever to enter the circle, armed or not. If *he* didn't care about appearances, no one else could afford to comment.

But Sola had at least been faithful to her chosen husbands, except for a little funny business at the very beginning with that Sos fellow. What was she doing now, wandering about with a (hitherto) nameless youth?

"The Master trained him," she said. "He wanted him to take his name by himself, without prejudice."

A protege of the Weaponless! That made several things fall into place. Well trained naturally; the Master knew all weapons as adversaries. Strong, yes, that followed. Ugly, of course. This was exactly the sort of man the Nameless One would like. Perhaps this was what the Master himself had been like as a youth.

And then he made another connection. "That wild boy that ravaged the crops five years ago——"

"Yes. A man, now."

Tyl's hands went to his own sticks. "He bit me then. I will have vengeance on him now."

"No," she said. "That is why I came. You shall not take Var to the circle."

"Is he afraid to meet me by day? I will waive terms."

"Var is afraid of nothing. But he is novice yet, and you the second ranked of the empire. He returns with me."

"He requires a woman to protect him?"

She stood up straight, her figure blooming like that of a freshly nubile girl. "Do you wish to answer to my husband?"

And Tyl, because he was bonded to the man she termed her husband, and was himself a man of honor, had to stifle his fury and answer no.

She turned to Var. "We'll stay the night here, then begin the journey back tomorrow. You will want to take your bracelet to the main tent."

Tyl smiled to himself. The new warrior, with his grotesqueries, would find no takers for his band. Let him celebrate alone!

And perhaps one day, one year, they would meet again, when the protection of the Nameless One did not apply. . . .

CHAPTER 5

Var knew well enough the significance of the golden bracelet. It was the product of crazy workmanship and distribution, costing the wearer nothing, indistinguishable physically from thousands of others. But not only did it identify him as a man, it served as a license to have a woman, for a night or a year or a lifetime. He had but to put the bracelet on the slender wrist of the girl of his choice and she was his, provided she agreed. Most girls were said to be flattered to be offered such attention, and sought to retain the bracelet as long as possible. They were particularly pleased to bear sons by the bracelet, for as a man proved himself in the circle, so a woman proved herself in fertility. The land always needed more people.

The big tent was standard. Each camp had one, where the unattached warriors resided and where single girls made themselves available. In winter a great fire heated the central chamber, while the couples occupying the fringe compartments trusted to sleeping bags and mutual warmth for their comfort.

Var was sure he would get by nicely on the latter system. In any event, it was summer.

Dusk, and the lamps were already lighted inside. The collective banquet was just finishing. Var, flush with his achievement of a name, had not been hungry, so that was no loss.

The girls were there, lounging on homemade furniture. The crazies provided everything a warrior might need but it was considered gauche to use such unearned merchandise. The nomads generally preferred to do for themselves.

He walked up to the nearest girl. She wore a lovely one-piece wraparound fastened in front with a silver brooch, the

24

costume signifying her availability. Her hair was a languorous waving brown. Her figure was excellent: high-breasted, low-thighed. Yes, she would do.

He looked the question at her, putting his right hand on the bracelet and beginning to twist it off. This was approved technique; he had seen warriors do it at the Master's camp.

"No," she said.

Var stopped, hand on wrist. Had he misunderstood? He was tempted to query her again but preferred not to speak. Words were not supposed to be necessary. He had only learned, or perhaps relearned, the language since joining the Master, and though he understood it well enough, his mouth and tongue did not form the syllables well.

He went on to the next somewhat disgruntled. He had not considered refusal and didn't know how to handle it. This adjacent girl was slightly younger, fair-haired and in pink. Now that he thought about it, she really looked better than the first. He tapped his bracelet.

She looked at him casually. "Can't you talk?"

Embarrassed, he grunted the word. "Brach-rit." Bracelet. It was clear in his mind.

"Get lost, stupid."

Var did not know how to deal with this either, so he nodded and went on.

None of the girls were interested. Some showed their contempt with disconcerting candor.

Finally an older woman wearing a bracelet came up to him. "You obviously don't understand, warrior, so I'll explain it to you. I saw you fight today, so don't think I'm trying to insult you."

Var was glad to have anyone treat him with respect. Gratefully, he listened to her.

"These girls are young," she said. "They have never had to work, they have never borne children, they have little experience. They're out for a good time. You—well, you're a stranger, so they're cautious. And you're a fledgling warrior, so they're contemptuous. Unjustly so. But as I said, they're young. And—I have to tell you—you're not pretty to look at. That doesn't matter in the circle, but it does here. An experienced woman might understand, but not these good-time juniors. Don't blame them. They need tempering by time, just as a warrior does. They make mistakes too."

Var nodded, frustrated but thankful for her advice, though he did not completely understand it. "Who——"

"I'm Tyla, the chief's wife. I just wanted you to understand."

He had meant to ask what girl to solicit next but was glad to know the identity of this helpful woman.

"Go back to your home camp, where they know you," she said. "Tyl doesn't like you, and that also prejudices your case here. I'm sorry to spoil your big night, but that's the way it is."

Now he understood. He wasn't wanted here. "Tanks," he said.

"Good luck, warrior. You'll find one who's right for you, and she'll be worth the wait. You have lost nothing here."

Var walked out of the tent.

Only as the cooling night air brushed him did the reaction come. *He was not wanted.* At the Master's camp he had been kindly treated, and no one had told him he was ugly. He had seemed to fit in with human life, despite his childhood in the wilderness. Now he knew that he had been sheltered, not physically, but socially. Today, with his formal achievement of manhood, he was also exposed to the truth. He was still a wild boy, unfit to mingle with human beings.

First he was embarrassed, so that his head was hot, his hands shaking. He had been blithely offering his shiny virgin bracelet.

Then he was furious. Why had he been subjected to this? What right had these tame pretty people to pass judgment on him? He tried to accommodate himself to their rules, and they rejected him. None of them would survive in the badlands!

He took out his shiny metal sticks and hefted them fondly. He was good with these. He was a warrior now. He needed to accept insults from no one. He stepped into the circle, the same one in which he had won his manhood earlier in the day. He waved his weapon.

"Come fight me!" he cried, knowing the words came out as gibberish but not caring. "I challenge you all!"

A man emerged from a small tent. "What's the noise?" he demanded. It was Tyl, the camp chief, dressed in a rough woolen nightshirt. The man who for some reason did not like Var. Var had never seen him before, that he recalled— though the man could have been among the crowds of people that had gawked at him when the Master first brought him from the badlands.

"What are you doing?" Tyl demanded, coming close. A yellow topknot dangled against the side of his head.

"Come fight me!" Var shouted, waving his sticks threateningly. His words might be incoherent, but his meaning could not be mistaken.

Tyl looked angry, but he did not enter the circle. "There is no fighting after dark," he said. "And if there were, I would not meet you, much as it would give me pleasure to bloody your ugly head and send you howling back through the cornfields. Stop making a fool of yourself."

Cornfields? Var almost made a connection.

Other people gathered, men and women and excited children. They peered through the gloom at Var, and he realized that he was now a far more ludicrous figure than he had been in the tent.

"Leave him alone," Tyl said and returned to his residence with an almost comical flirt of his topknot. The others dispersed, and soon Var was standing by himself again. He had only made things worse by his belligerence.

Dejected, he went to the only place he knew where he could find some understanding, however cynical: the isolated tent of his traveling companion, the Master's wife.

"I was afraid it would come to this," Sola said, her voice oddly soft. "I will go to Tyl and have him fetch you a damsel. You shall not be deprived this night."

"No!" Var cried, horrified that he should have to be satisfied by the intercession of a woman going to his enemy. Human mores were not natural to him, but this was too obviously a thing of shame.

"That, too, I anticipated," she said philosophically. "That's why I had my tent set up away from the main camp."

Var did not understand.

"Come in, lie down," she said. "It's not as bad as you think. A man doesn't prove himself in one day or one night; it's the years that show the truth."

Var crawled into the tent and lay down beside her. He really did not know this woman well. She had remained aloof all the years the Master trained him, only instructing him curtly in computations. Thanks to her, he could count to one hundred and tell whether six handfuls of four ears of corn were more than two baskets with fifteen ears each. (They were not.) Such calculations were difficult and pointless; he had not enjoyed the lessons, and Sola had made him feel particularly stupid, but the Master had insisted. Thus his chief association with her had been negative.

He had been surprised when she was delegated—or had volunteered—to accompany him here for his manhood test. A woman! But as it had turned out, she was quite competent. She walked well, so that they made good distance each day, and knew the route, and when they encountered strangers she had done the talking. They had spent the nights in the hostels, she in one bunk, he in another, though he would have preferred even now to sleep in a familiar tree. She remained aloof, but she did not entirely conceal her body as she showered and changed for the night, and the glimpses he had had had given him painful erections. His nature was animal; *any* female, even one as old as this, provoked him. And she did know his origin and understand his limitations.

Now, in this strange unfriendly camp, hurt by his own failures, he had come to her, his only contact with his only friend, the Master.

"So you asked the young girls, and they ridiculed you," she said. "I had hoped better for you, but I was young once myself, and just as narrow. I thought power was most important, to marry a chief. And so I lost the man I loved, and now I am sorry."

She had never talked like this before. Var lay silent, satisfied for the moment to listen. It was better than thinking of his own humiliations. She referred, of course, to her former husband, Sol of All Weapons, who had lost his empire to the Master and had gone to the mountain with his baby girl. The episode had become legend already; everyone knew of that momentous transfer of power and that tragic father-daughter suicide.

If Sola had loved power so much that she had given up the man she loved and the daughter she had borne to him, and taken the victor to her bed, no wonder she suffered!

"Would you understand," she asked, "if I told you that when I thought I'd lost my love forever, he returned to me, and I found that it was only his body, not his heart, that was mine, and even that body maimed and unfamiliar?"

"No," Var said honestly. It was easier to voice the words for her, for she understood him whether or not his wilderness mouth cooperated.

"Not everything is what it seems," she murmured. "You too will find that friendship can make hard requirements of you, and those you might deem enemy are men to be trusted. Life is like that. Come, let's get this done with."

He recognized a dismissal and began to crawl out of the tent.

"No," she said gently, holding him back. "This is your night, and you shall have it in full measure. I will be your woman."

Var made a gutteral sound, dumbfounded. Could he have understood her correctly?

"Sorry, Var," she said. "I spoke too abruptly. Lie down."

He lay down again.

"Wild boy," she continued, "you are not a man until you have taken a woman. So it is written in our unwritten code. I came to make sure you accomplished it all. I have"—here she paused—"done this before. Long ago. My husband knows. Believe me, Var, though this appears to be a violation of the standards we have taught you, this is the way it must be. I cannot explain it further. But you must understand one thing, and promise me another."

He had to speak. "The Master—"

"Var, *he knows!*" she whispered fiercely. "But he will never speak of it. This was decided almost ten years ago. And you must know this, too: I am older than you, but I am not past bearing age. The Nameless One is sterile. Tonight and the nights that follow—it ends when we reach home camp—if you should beget a child on me, it will be the child of the Weaponless. I will never wear your bracelet. I will never touch you again after this journey. I will never speak of what happened here between us, and neither will you. If I am pregnant, you will be sent away. You have no claim upon me. It will be as though it never happened, except that you will be a man. Do you understand?"

"No, no . . ." he mumbled, already sick with lust for her.

"You understand." She reached out suddenly and put her hand upon his loin. "You understand."

He understood that she was offering her body to him, and that he had no stamina to refuse. He was wilderness-bred; the willingness of the female was the male's command.

"But you must promise me," she said as she took his clubbed hand, only recently capable of any gentleness, and brought it to her tender breast. She was already nude within her bag. "You must promise. . . ."

The heat was rising in him, abolishing any scruples he might have had. Var knew he would do it. Perhaps the Master would kill him, but tonight . . .

"You must promise *to kill the man who harms my child.*"

Var went chill. "You have no child!" he blurted. "None that can be harmed." And he became aware again of his crudity and cruelty of word and concept. He was still wild.

"Promise."

"How can I promise when your child is long dead?"

She silenced him with the first fully female kiss he had ever experienced. "If ever the situation arises, you will know," she said.

"I promise." What else could he do?

She said no more, but her body spoke for her, this supposedly aloof, cold woman. Novice that he was, Var still recognized in her a fury of unprecedented proportion. She was hot, she was lithe, she was savage. She was at least twenty-five years old, but in the dark she seemed a buxom eager fifteen. It was not hard to forget for the moment that she was in fact middle-aged.

As the connection was made and the explosion formed within him, he realized that it might be his own future child he had just sworn to avenge . . . anonymously.

CHAPTER 6

The Master was waiting for them. He used one of the crazy hostels as a business office and had entire drawers of papers with writing on them. Var had never comprehended the reason for such records, but he did not question the wisdom of his mentor. The Master was literate: He was able to look at the things called books and repeat speeches that men long dead had said. This was an awesome yet useless ability.

"Here is your warrior," Sola said. "Var the Stick—a man in every sense of the word." And with an obscure smile she departed for her own tent.

The Master stood in the glassy rotating door of the cylindrical hostel and studied Var for a long moment. "Yes, you are changed. Do you know now what it is to keep a secret? To know and not speak?"

Var nodded affirmatively, thinking of what had passed between him and the Master's phenomenal wife on the way home. Even if he had not been forbidden to talk of that, he would have balked at this point.

"I have another secret for you. Come." And with no further question or explanation the Nameless One led the way away from the cabin, letting the door spin about behind him. Var glanced once more at the sparkling, transparent cone that topped the hostel and its mysterious mechanisms, and turned to follow.

They walked a mile, passing warriors and their families busy at sundry tasks—practicing with weapons, mending clothing, cleaning meat—and exchanged routine greetings.

31

The Master seemed to be in no hurry. "Sometimes," he said, "a man can find himself in a situation not of his making or choosing, where he must keep silence even though he prefers to speak, and though others may deem him a coward. But his preference is not always wise, and the opinion of others does not make a supposition true. There is courage of other types than that of the circle."

Var realized that his friend was telling him something important, but he wasn't sure how it applied. He sensed that the Master's secret was going to be as important to his life as Sola's had been to his manhood. Strange things seemed to be developing; the situation was changed from his prior experience.

When they were well beyond the sight or hearing of any other person, the Master cut away from the beaten trail and began to run. He galloped ponderously, shaking the ground, and his breath emerged noisily, but he maintained a good pace. Var ran with him, far more easily, mystified. The Master, as he well knew, was tireless—but where was he going?

Their route led toward the local badlands markers, then along them, then through them. Var had thought the Weaponless was afraid of such regions, since his severe radiation sickness of the time the two had met. It had taken the man months to regain his full strength; and from time to time, in the privacy of tent or office, he had bled again or been sick or reeled from surges of weakness. Var knew this well, and Sola was aware of it, but it had been hidden from others of the empire. Much of the early battle training Var had received had been as much to exercise the Master gradually as to profit the wild boy. And it had been common knowledge that the Master avoided the badlands with almost cowardly care.

Obviously he was *not* afraid. Why had he let men think he was? Was this what he had referred to just now, that other kind of courage? But what reason could there be for it?

Deep in the badlands, but in a place where there was no radiation, there was a camp. Strange warriors manned it, men Var had never seen before. They wore funny green clothing riddled with knobs and pockets, and on their heads were inverted pots. They carried metal rocks.

The leader of this odd tribe came up promptly. He was short, stout, old, and had curly yellow hair. Obviously unfit to fight in the circle. "This is Jim," the Master said. "Var the Stick," he added, completing the introduction.

The two men eyed each other suspiciously.

"Jim and Var," the Master said, smiling grimly, "you don't know each other, but I want you to accept my word on this: You can trust each other. You both have had similar misfortunes—Jim whose brother of the same name went to the mountain twenty years ago, Var whose whole family was lost in the badlands."

Var still was not impressed, and the other man seemed to share his sentiment. To be without family was no signal of merit.

"Var is a warrior I have personally trained. His skin is immediately sensitive to radiation, so that he cannot accidentally be burned, no matter where he goes."

Jim became intensely interested.

"And Jim—Jim the Gun, if you want his weapon—is literate. He and I made contact by letter years ago, when the . . . the need developed. He has studied the old texts and knows as much as any man among the nomads about explosive weapons. He is training this group in the ancient techniques of warfare."

Var recognized the man's weapon now. It was one of the metal stones that were stored in certain badlands buildings. But it hardly seemed suitable for use in the circle. It had no cutting edge and was far too small and clumsy to serve as a club. And once thrown, it would be lost.

"Var will be liaison man between this group and the outside," the Master said. "Assuming he is willing. Later he'll be an advance scout. But I want him to know how to shoot, too."

Jim and Var still merely looked at each other. "I'll break the ice," the Master said. "Then I'll have to go back before someone misses me. Var, fetch that jug over there, if you please." He pointed across a field to a brown ceramic jar perched on an old stump.

Jim started to say something, but the Master held up his hand. Var loped toward the stump. About half the way he skidded to a stop. His skin was burning. He retreated a few paces and circled to the side, looking for a way around the radiation.

It took him several minutes, but finally he found a channel

and reached the jug. He brought it back, retracing his devious route. The master and Jim had been joined by a dozen other men, all watching silently.

Var handed over the jug.

"It's true! A living geiger!" Jim exclaimed, amazed. "We can use him, all right."

The Master returned the jug to Var. "Set it on the ground about fifty feet away, if you please."

Var complied.

"Demonstrate your shotgun," the Master said to him.

The man went into a tent and brought out an object like a sheathed sword. He held it up, pointing the narrow end toward the jug.

"There will be noise," the Master warned Var. "It will not harm you. I suggest you watch the jug."

Var did so. Suddenly a blast of thunder occurred beside him, making him jump and grab for his weapon. The distant jug shattered as though smashed by a club. No one had touched it or thrown anything at it.

"Pieces of metal from this long gun did that," the Master said. "Jim will show you how it works. Stay with him, as you choose; I will return another day." And he left, cantering as before.

Jim turned to Var. "How is it that you are not bonded, since he trained you himself and trusts you with this secret?"

Var did not answer immediately. He had not realized it before, but it was true he was not bonded. He was not a member of the Nameless One's empire or any of its subject tribes, for he had never been defeated in the circle. His only battle had been the formal achievement of his manhood. Ordinarily a warrior joined a tribe of his choosing by ritually challenging its chief. When he lost—as was inevitable, for no novice could match a chief—he was according to nomad convention bonded, subject to the will of that leader or the leader's leader. If he fought a man from another tribe and lost, his allegiance changed; if he won, the other man joined his own tribe. Once Var had taken name and bracelet, he had become a free agent, until such time as he lost that freedom in the circle.

Why had the Weaponless never made arrangement for Var? And how had Jim known about this omission?

"He was scrupulous about saying 'if you please' to you," Jim said. "That meant he could not order you."

"I . . . don't know why," Var said. Then, seeing the perplexity on the man's face, he repeated it more carefully, forcing his tongue to get it right. "Don't . . . know."

"Well, it's none of my business," Jim said easily, pretending not to notice Var's clumsiness with the language. "I won't bother with that formality of address; if I tell you to do something, it's not an order, only advice. Okay?"

"Okay," Var said, able to pronounce these syllables well enough.

"And I'll have to tell you a lot, because guns are dangerous. They can kill just as readily as a sword can, and do it from a distance. You saw the jug."

Var had seen the jug. What could shatter it at fifty feet should be able to hurt a man at the same distance.

Jim put his hand on the metal at his hip. "Here—first lesson. This is a pistol, a small handgun. One of the hundreds we found stored in boxes in a badlands building. We had to use the click-boxes to chart a route in; I don't know how the boss knew about it. I've been running this camp for the past three years, training the men he sends . . . but that's beside the point." He did something, and the metal opened. "It's hollow, see. This is the barrel. And this is a bullet. You put the bullet in here, close it up, and when you press this trigger—blam! The bullet explodes, and part of it shoots out here, very fast. It's like a thrown dagger. Watch."

He set up a piece of wood, pointed the hollow end of the pistol at it and shoved his forefinger against the spike he called the trigger. "Noise," he warned, and there was a burst of sound. Smoke shot out of the gun, and the wood jumped.

Jim broke open the weapon, that now seemed to be hot, and showed Var the interior. "See, bullet's gone. And if you'll look at the target—that piece of wood—you'll see where it hit." He offered the weapon to Var. "Now you try it."

Var accepted the gun, and after some struggle got a bullet in. But his hand would not fit around the base properly, and his finger was too thick and warped to maneuver the trigger. Jim, perceiving the difficulty as quickly as Var did, quickly produced a larger gun. This one Var managed to fire.

The shock traveled up his arm, but it was slight compared to the tap of a stick in the circle. His bullet plowed into the ground. "We'll show you how to aim," Jim said. "Remember, the gun *is* a weapon, but unlike the instruments you are familiar with, it can kill by accident. Treat it as you would a sword in motion. With respect."

Var learned a great deal in the following days. He had thought there was little more to discover, after Sola had shown him the marvelous social intricacies of generating life. Now he wondered that anything at all remained, as Jim showed him the devastating unsocial devices for terminating life.

The Master came for him. "Now you know part of my secret," he said. "And I will tell you another part. This is an invasion force, and we shall invade the mountain."

"The mountain!"

"The mountain of death, yes. It is not what you have supposed, what all nomads suppose. Not every man who goes there dies. There are people living beneath it, similar to the crazies, but with guns. They hold hostages——" But here he changed his mind. "We must storm that mountain and drive out these men. Only then will the empire be secure."

"I don't understand." Actually, it was a questioning grunt.

"I have held the empire in check for six years, because I feared the power of the underworld. Now I am ready to move against it. I do not say that these are evil men, but they must be displaced. Once that enemy is gone, the empire will expand rapidly, and we shall bring civilization to all the continent."

So the murmurings of discontent had been wrong there too! The Weaponless was *not* stifling the empire, not permanently.

"I have a dangerous assignment for you. I have left you a free agent so that you may choose for yourself. It will require working alone, going into extremely unpleasant places, and telling no one of your mission or your adventures except me. I told Jim you were to be liaison man and scout, but this is dangerous scouting he doesn't know about. You may die violently, but not in the circle. You may be tortured. You may be trapped in lethal radiation. You may have to violate the code of the circle in order to succeed, for we are dealing with unscrupulous men. The leader of the underworld has only contempt for our mores and our honor."

The Master waited, but Var did not reply.

"You may ask what you want in return. I mean to deal fairly with you."

"After I do this," Var enunciated carefully, "then can I join the empire?"

The Nameless One looked at him, astonished. Then he began to laugh. Var laughed too, not certain what was funny.

CHAPTER 7

The beginning was only a hole in a pit in a cavity in the ground, where water disappeared during storms. But underneath it expanded into a cavern he could almost stand in. Var remained there for a time, motionless, getting his full night vision and absorbing the smells.

He knew in which direction the mountain lay. This sense, like that of smell and his sharp night sight and his ability to run almost doubled over, had remained with him after he left the wild life. He was still quite at home in the wilderness.

He shook off his shoes. He had never been comfortable in them, and for this work his hooflike toes were best.

Some water still seeped down, but the main section of the cave was clear. The base was caked with gravel; the sides were slimy with mosslike fungus. On a hunch abetted by observation, Var took a singlestick and scraped the wall. As the life and grime gave way, metal touched metal.

This cave was not completely natural. The Master had suggested that this might be the case. The entire mountain, he had said, was unnatural, though he did not know how it had come about.

The chances of an unnatural cave connecting to an unnatural mountain seemed good.

His eyes, ears and nose now adjusted to this environment, Var moved on. His mission was to chart a route into the dread mountain, a route that bypassed the surface defenses and that men could follow. If he found the route, and kept it secret from the underworlders, the empire could have an almost bloodless victory. If there were no route, there would be a much worse battle on the surface. Lives depended on his mission, perhaps the life of the Master himself.

38

The tunnel branched. The pipe going toward the mountain was clogged with rubble; the other was wide and clear. Var knew why: When rainfall was heavy, water coursed this way, removing all obstructions. He would have to follow the water to be sure of getting anywhere, but he would also have to pay close attention to the weather, lest the water follow *him.* Was it possible to anticipate a storm . . . underground?

The passage widened as it descended. Its walls were metallic and almost vertical; overhead, metal beams now showed regularly. It debouched into an extremely large concourse with a long pit down the center. Var peered down, noting how the delta of rubble tipped into that chasm. He did not venture into it himself. The bottom was packed with slick-looking mud, and there were dark motions within that mud: worms, maggots or worse. There had been a time when he had eaten such with gusto, but civilization had affected his appetite.

He tapped the level surface of the upper platform. Under the crusted grime there was tile very like that of a hostel. The footing was sound.

The Master had told him that there were many artifacts in this region remaining from the time before the Blast. The Ancients had made buildings and tunnels and miraculous machines, and some of these remained, though no one knew their function. Certainly Var could not fathom the use of such a large, long compartment with a tiled floor and a pit dividing it completely.

He followed it down, listening to distant rustles and sniffing the stale drifts of air. Though his eyes were fully adapted to the gloom, he could not see clearly for any distance. There was not enough light for any proper human vision this deep in the bowel.

Soon the platform narrowed, and finally the wall slanted into the pit, and there was nowhere to go but down. The Ancients could not have used this for walking, then, since it went nowhere. They had been, the Master said, like the crazies and like the underworlders, only more so; there was no fathoming their motives. This passage proved it. To put such astonishing labors into so useless a structure. . . .

He climbed down carefully. The drop was only a few feet, not hazardous in itself. It was the life in that lower muck that he was wary of. Familiar, it might be harmless, as familiar

poison berries were harmless—no one would eat them. Unfamiliar, it was potentially deadly.

But the mud was harder than he had supposed; the gloom
had changed its seeming properties. Rising from it were two
narrow metal rails side by side but several feet apart. They
were quite firm, refusing to bend or move no matter what
pressure he applied, and they extended as far as he could
discern along the pit. He found that by balancing on one he
could walk along without touching the mud at all, and that
was worthwhile.

He moved. His hoof-toes, softened some by the shoes he
had had to wear among men but still sturdy, pounded rapidly
on the metal as he got the feel of it, and his balance
became sure despite the darkness and the slender support.
The pit of the tunnel was interminable and did not go toward
the mountain. He hesitated to go too far lest a rainstorm
develop above and send its savage waters down to drown
him before he could escape. Then he realized that this tunnel
was too large to fill readily, and saw the dusky watermarks
on its cold walls, only two or three feet above the level
of the rails. He could wade or swim if it came to that.

Even so, it was pointless to follow this passage indefinitely.
It was now curving farther away from the mountain, so could
hardly serve the Master's purpose.

He would follow it another five minutes or so, then turn
back.

But in one minute he was stopped. The tunnel ended.
Rather, something was blocking it. A tremendous metal plug,
with spurs and gaps and rungs.

Var tapped it with his stick. The thing was hollow, but
firm. It seemed to rest on the rails, humping up somewhat
between them so as not to touch the floor.

Could there be a branching or turning beyond this obstacle?
Var grabbed hold and hauled himself up the face of the
plug, curling his fingers stiffly around what offered. He was
searching to learn whether there were a way through it.

There was. He poked his head into the musty interior,
inhaling the stale air. He knocked on the side of the square
aperture and it clanged. He could tell the surrounding configuration of metal by the sound and echo. He climbed inside.

The floor here was higher than outside. It was mired in a
thick layer of dirt and droppings. This was like a badlands
building, with places that could be seats, and other places that

could be windows, except that there was only a brief space between the apertures and the blank tunnel wall. And all of it was dark. His eyes useless, his ears becoming confused by the confinement of sound, Var finally had to use the crazy flashlight the Master had given him. For there was life here.

Something stirred. Var suppressed a reflexive jump and put the beam of light on it, shielding his eyes somewhat from the intolerable glare. Then he got smart and clapped his hand over the plastic lens, holding in the light so that only red welts glowed through. He aimed, let digits relax, let the beam shove out to spear its prey.

It was a rat, a blotched, small-eyed creature that shied away from the brilliance with a squeal of pain.

This Var knew: rats did not travel alone. Where one could live, a hundred could live. And where rats resided, so did predators. Probably small ones—weasels, mink, mongoose— but possibly numerous. And the rats themselves could be vicious and sometimes rabid, as he knew from badlands buildings.

He walked quickly down the long, narrow room, seeing a doorway at its end outlined by the finger-modulated beam. He had to move along before too many creatures gathered. Rats did not stay frightened long without reason.

Beyond the door was a kind of chamber, and another door. More mysterious construction by the Ancients!

Coming down the hall beyond that was a snake. A large one, several feet long. Not poisonous, he judged, but unfamiliar and possibly mutant. He retreated.

The rats were already massed in the other room. Var strode through them, shining his light where he intended to step, and they skittered back. But they closed in behind, little teeth showing threateningly, too aggressive for his comfort. He had stirred up an ugly nest, and they were bold in their own territory.

He scrambled out the window and dropped to the dank floor of the tunnel. His feet sank into the mud; it was softer here, or he had broken through a crust. He turned off the flash, waited a moment to recover sight and found a rail to follow back down the tunnel.

Some other way would have to be found. It was not that the rats and snakes stopped him, but there were sure to be other animals, and a troop of men would stir them all up. In any event, the direction was wrong.

But he could not escape the angry stir so easily. Something silent came down the tunnel. He felt the moving air and ducked nervously. It was a bat, the first of many.

What did all these creatures feed on? There seemed to be no green plants, only mold and fungus. And insects. Now he heard them stirring, rising into the foul air from their myriad burrows.

Apprehensively, he flashed his light.

Some were white moths.

Var's heart thudded. There was no way he could be sure of avoiding these deadly stingers here except by standing still —and that had its own dangers. He had to move, and if he brushed into one . . . well, he would have a couple of hours to reach the surface and seek help before the poison brought him to a full and possibly fatal coma. Certainly fatal if he succumbed to it here in the tunnels, where men would never find him. Even if he received only a minor sting, that weakened him, and then it rained . . . or if the rats and snakes became more bold, and ventured along the rail. . . .

But not all white moths were badlands mutants. These seemed smaller. Maybe they were innocuous.

If these were of the deadly variety, this route was doomed. Men could not use it, however directly it might lead to the mountain. That would make further exploration useless.

Best to know immediately. Var ran along the track until he saw the high platforms. He climbed up and oriented himself, identifying his original point of entry. Then he ran after a white moth and swooped with his two hands, trapping it. It was his fingers that were awkward, not his wrists or hands.

He held the insect cupped clumsily between his palms, terrified yet determined. For thirty seconds he stood there, controlling his quivering, sweating digits.

The moth fluttered in its prison, but Var felt no sting. He squeezed it gently and it struggled softly.

At last he opened his hands and let the creature go. It was harmless.

Then he rested for five minutes, regaining his equilibrium. He would much rather have stepped into the circle with lame hands against a master sworder than against a badlands moth like this. But he had made the trial and won. The way was still clear.

He crossed the double-rail pit and mounted to the far platform. There were tunnels leading away in the proper direction. He chided himself for not observing them before. He selected one and ran down it.

And halted. His skin was burning.

There was radiation here. Intense.

He backed off and tried another branch. Even sooner he encountered it. Impassable.

He tried a third. This went farther, but eventually ran into the same wall of radiation. It was as though the mountain were ringed by roentgen.

That left the railed tunnel, going in the other direction. This might circle around the flesh-rotting rays. He had to know.

Var dropped down and ran along the track. He went faster than before, because time had been consumed in the prior explorations, and he had greater confidence in the narrow footing. Probably a man with normal, soft, wide feet could not have stayed on the track so readily. Or have felt its continuing solidity by the tap of nail on metal, an important reassurance in this gloom.

The tunnel curved toward the mountain.

On and on it went, for miles. He passed another series of platforms, and felt the barest tinge of radiation; just before he stopped on the track it faded, and he went on. Such a level of the invisible death was not good to stay in but was harmless for a rapid passage.

The rubble between the tracks became greater, the walls more ragged, as though some tremendous pressure had pressed and shaken this region. He had seen such collapsed structures during his wild-boy years; now he wondered whether the rubble and the radiation could be connected in any way. But this was idle speculation.

He was very near the mountain now. He came to a third widening of the tunnel and platform, but this one was in very bad condition. Tumbled stone was everywhere, and some radiation. He ran on by, nervous about the durability of this section. A badlands building in such disrepair was prone to collapse on small provocation, and here the falling rock would be devastating.

But the track stopped. It twisted about, unsettling him unexpectedly (he should have paid attention to its changing beat under his toes!), and terminated in a ragged spire. Beyond that the rubble filled in the tunnel until there was no room to pass.

Var went back to the third set of platforms. He crawled
up on the mountainside, avoiding rubble and alert to any
sensation in his skin. When he felt the radiation, even so
slight as to be harmless, he shied away. The Master had
stressed that a route entirely clear must be found, for ordinary men might be more sensitive to the rays than Var, despite their inability to detect it without click-boxes.

Two passages were invisibly sealed off. The third was clear,
barely. There were large droppings in it, showing that the
animals had already discovered its availability. This in turn
suggested that it went somewhere, perhaps to the surface, for
the animals would not travel so frequently in and out of a
dead end.

It branched—the Ancients must have had trouble making
up their minds!—and again he took the fork leading toward
the mountain. And again he ran into trouble.

For this was the lair of an animal, a large one. The droppings here were ponderous and fresh, the fruit of a carni-
vore. Now he smelled its rank body effusions, and now he
heard its tread.

But the tunnel was high and clear, and he could run
swiftly along it. It was narrow enough so that any creature
could come at him only from front or back. So he waited
for it, impelled by curiosity. If it were something that could
be killed to clear the passage for human infiltration of the
mountain, he would make the report. He cupped the light
and aimed it ahead.

Rats scuttled around a bend, squinted in the glare and
milled in confusion. Then a gross head appeared: froglike,
large-eyed, horny-beaked. The mouth opened toothlessly.
There was a flash of pink. A rat squealed and bounced up,
then was drawn by a pink strand into that orifice. It was an
extensive, sticky tongue that did the hauling.

The beam played over one bulging eye, and the creature
blinked and twisted aside. It seemed to be a monstrous sala-
mander. As Var stepped back, some fifteen feet of its body
came into sight. The skin was flexible, glistening; the legs
were squat, the tail was stout.

Var wasn't certain he could kill it with his sticks, but he
was sure he could hurt it and drive it back. This was an
amphibian mutant. The moist skin and flipperlike extremities
suggested that it spent much time in water. And his skin
reacted to its presence: The creature was slightly radioactive.

That meant that there was water, probably a flooded tunnel, water that extended into radiation and was contaminated by it. And there would be other such mutants, for no creature existed alone. This was not a suitable route for man.

Var turned and ran, not fearing the creature but not caring to stay near it either. It was a rat eater and probably beneficial to man in that sense. He had no reason to fight it.

That left the other fork of the passage. He turned into it and trotted along, feeling the press of time more acutely. He was hungry, too. He wished he could unroll his tongue and spear something tasty many feet away and suck it in. Man didn't have all the advantages.

There was another cave-in, but he was able to scramble through. And on the far side there was light.

Not daylight. The yellow glow of an electric bulb. He had reached the mountain.

The passage was clean here and wide. Solid boxes were stacked in piles, providing cover. This had to be a storeroom.

Near the opening through which he had entered there was food: several chunks of bread, a dish of water.

Poison! his mind screamed. He had avoided such traps many times in the wild state. Anything set out so invitingly and inexplicably was suspect. This would be how the underworlders kept the rats down.

He had accomplished his mission. He could return and lead the troops here, with their guns. This chamber surely opened into the main areas of the mountain, and there was room here for the men to mass before attacking.

Still—he had better make quite sure, for it would be very bad if by some fluke the route were closed beyond this point. He moved deeper into the room, hiding behind the boxes though there was no one to see him. At the far end he discovered a closed door. He approached it cautiously. He touched the strange knob. . . .

And heard footsteps.

Var started for the tunnel but realized almost immediately that he could not get through the small aperture unobserved in the time he had. He ducked behind the boxes again as the knob rotated and the door opened. He could wait, and if discovered he could kill the man and be on his way. He hefted his two sticks, afraid to peek around lest he expose himself.

The steps came toward him, oddly light and quick. To check the poison, he realized suddenly. The food would have to be replaced every few hours, or the rats would foul it and ignore it. As the person passed him, Var poked his head over between shielding flaps and looked.

It was a woman.

His grip tightened on the sticks. How could he kill a woman? Only men fought in the circle. Women were not barred from it specifically; they merely lacked the intelligence and skill required for such activity, and of course their basic function was to support and entertain the men. And if he did kill her, what would he do with the body? A corpse was hard to conceal for long, because it began to smell. It would betray his presence if not immediately certainly within hours. Far too soon for the nomads to enter secretly.

She was middle-aged, though of smaller build than the similarly advanced woman he had known, Sola. Her hair was short, brown and curly, but her face retained an elfin quality and she moved with grace. She wore a smock that concealed her figure; had her face and poise not given her away, Var might have mistaken her for a child because of her diminutive stature. Was this what all underworlders were like? Small and old and smocked? No need to worry about the conquest, then.

She glanced at the bread, then beyond—and stopped.

There, in the scant dust, was Var's footprint. The round, callused ball, the substantial, protective, curled-under toenails. She might not recognize it as human, but she had to realize that something much larger than a rat had passed.

Var charged her, both sticks lifted. He had no choice now.

She whirled to face him, raising her small hands. Somehow his sticks missed her head . . . and he was wrenched about, half-lifted, stumbling into the wall, twisting, falling.

He caught his footing again and oriented on her. He saw her fling off her smock and stand waiting for him, hands poised, body balanced, expression alert. She wore a brief skirt and briefer halter and was astonishingly feminine in contour for her age. Again, like Sola.

He had seen that wary, competent attitude before. When the Master had captured him in the badlands. When men faced each other in the circle. It was incredible that a woman, one past her prime and hardly larger than a child, should show such readiness. But he had learned to deal with oddities and to read the portents rapidly and accurately.

He turned again and scrambled into the tunnel.

On the dark side he rolled over and waited with the sticks for her head to poke through the narrow aperture. But she was clever; she did not follow him. He risked one look back through and saw her standing still, watching.

Quickly he retreated. When he deemed it safe, he began to run, retracing his route. He had a report to make.

CHAPTER 8

The Master listened with complete passivity to the report.
Var was afraid he had failed but did not know quite how, for
he *had* found a route into the mountain. "So if she tells the
mountain master, they will seal up the passage. But we could
reopen it—"

"Not against a flamethrower," the Nameless One said mo-
rosely. Then, amazingly, he bent his head into his hands.
"Had I known! Had I known! *She,* of all people! I would
have gone myself!"

Var stared at him, not comprehending. "You recognize the
woman?"

"Sosa."

He waited, but the Master did not clarify the matter. The
name meant nothing to Var.

After a long time, the Weaponless spoke: "We shall have
to mount a direct frontal attack. Bring Tyl to me."

Var left without replying; Tyl was no friend of his, and
Tyl was in his own camp several hundred miles away. Var
did not *have* to follow any empire directive, but he would go
for Tyl.

Jim the Gun intercepted him as he departed. "Show him
this," he said. "No one else."

And he gave Var a handgun and a box of ammunition.
And a written note.

Tyl was impressed by power and therefore fascinated by
the gun. In some fashion Var did not follow, but which he
suspected was influenced by the note Tyl's wife read, the chief
set aside his standing grudge and cultivated Var for his
knowledge of firearms.

Var had good memory for any person who had ever

threatened his well-being, and he had not at all forgotten his embarrassments of the first meeting with this man. But Tyl was one of those who, though maddening when antipathetic, could be absolutely charming when friendly. As surely as he might have courted a lovely girl, Tyl courted Var.

And by the time Tyl and his vast tribe reached the mountain, he and Var were friends. They entered the circle together many times, but never for terms or blood, and under Tyl's expert guidance Var became far more proficient with the sticks. He saw that he had been a preposterous fool ever to challenge Tyl with this weapon; the man had never had cause to fear him in the circle. A dozen times in practice Tyl disarmed him, each time showing him the mistake he had made and drilling him in the proper countermoves.

Tyl named him a score of names, stickers of the empire, that were his marks to excell, and warned him of the other warriors to be wary of. "You are strong and tough," he said, "and courageous—but you still lack sufficient experience. In a year, two years. . . ."

Var, in those evenings when the tribe settled for the night and went about the processes even a traveling tribe must go about, also had regular practice against other weapons. The Master had instructed him in the basic techniques, but that was not at all the same as actual combat. The stick had to learn to blunt the sword, thwart the club and to navigate the staff—or the stick was useless. Here with Tyl's disciplined, combat-ready tribe, Var's stick mastered these things.

More of a warrior than he had been, he returned to the Nameless One's hidden camp near the mountain. Now he understood why Tyl was second in command. The man was honorable and sensible and capable and an expert warrior— and not given to letting minor grudges override his judgment. The feud between them had been a momentary thing that Var had mistaken once for malice. The Master must have known and shown him the truth by sending him on this mission.

Var was present when the Weaponless conferred with the Two Weapons.

"You have seen the gun," the Master said. "What it can do."

Tyl nodded. The truth was that he had fired it many times and become fairly proficient. He had even brought down a rabbit with it, something Var, with his clumsy grip, could not do.

"The men we face have guns and worse weapons. They do not honor the code of the circle."

Tyl nodded again. Var knew he was fascinated by the tactical problems inherent in gun combat.

"For six years I have held the empire in check, for fear of the killers of the underworld, their guns, when we had none."

Tyl looked surprised, realizing that this was not just a staging area. "The men who travel to the mountain—"

"Do not always die there."

Var did not comprehend the expression that crossed Tyl's face. "Sol of All Weapons . . ."

"There—alive. Hostage."

"And you—"

"I came from the mountain. I returned."

Now Tyl's mouth fell open. "Sos! Sos the rope! And the bird—"

"Nameless, weaponless, helpless. Stupid dead. Bound to dismantle the empire."

Tyl looked as though something astonishing and profound and not entirely pleasing had passed between them, more than the information about the mountain. Var could not quite grasp what, though he did recognize the name "Sos" as connected to "Sosa." He suspected that Tyl's most basic loyalty lay with Sol of All Weapons, the former master of the empire; perhaps the knowledge that that man lived made Tyl excited.

"Now—?" Tyl inquired.

"Now we also have guns."

"The empire—"

"Will expand. Perhaps under Sol, as before. After this conquest of the mountain."

"But these . . . guns . . . are not circle weapons," Tyl protested. Var could see how eager he was.

"This is not a circle matter. It is war."

Var was shocked. He knew what war was. The Master had told him many times. War was the cause of the Blast.

The Master glanced at him, fathoming his disturbance. "I have told you war is evil, that it must never come to our society. It very nearly destroyed the world once. But we are faced here with a problem that can not be allowed to stand. The mountain must be reduced. This is the war to end wars."

What the Master said seemed reasonable, but Var knew that something was wrong. There was evil in this project, and not the evil of war itself. For the first time he questioned the wisdom of the Weaponless. But he could not decide what it was that bothered him, so he said nothing.

Tyl did not look comfortable either, but he did not argue. "How are we to accomplish this?"

The Master brought out a sketch he must have made during the months of his encampment here. "This is what the crazies call a contour map. I have made sightings of the mountain from all sides, and the land about it. See—here is our present camp, well beyond its defensive perimeter. Here is the hostel where the suicides stop before making the ascent. Here is the subway tunnel Var explored."

"Subway?" Evidently the word was as new to Tyl as it was to Var.

"The Ancients used it for traveling. Metal vehicles something like crazy tractors, except that they rolled on tracks and moved much faster. The ones on the ground were called 'trains' and the ones below, 'subways.' Var tells me he discovered an actual train down there, too."

Var had told him no such thing. He had only reported on what he found: tunnels, platforms, rails, a plug, a cave-in, radiation, a monster. He had seen nothing like a crazy tractor. Why should the Master lie?

"I had hoped to use such a route to make a surprise foray. But the underworld knows of it now, knows that we know that the radiation is down. So they will have it booby-trapped. We must make an overland attack."

Tyl looked relieved. "My tribe will take it for you."

The Master smiled. "I do not question the competence of your tribe. But your men are warriors of the circle. What would they do against guns? Guns fired from cover, from a distance, without warning. And flamethrowers?"

"Flamethrowers?"

"Jets of fire that consume a man in moments."

Tyl nodded, but Var could see that he did not believe such a thing was possible, despite the other wonders they had learned about. Var didn't either. If fire were shot out in a jet the wind would put it out.

"Do you remember when someone told you about white moths whose sting was deadly? About tiny creatures who could overrun armed warriors? Fire that would float on water?"

"I remember," Tyl said, and was sober.

Var did not see what relevance such rhetorical questions had to the problem, since everyone knew about the moths and the swarming shrews of the badlands. Floating fire was ridiculous. But now Tyl seemed to believe in flamethrowers.

"This will be ugly fighting," the Weaponless said. "Men will die outside the circle never seeing the men who kill them. We are like the shrews; we must swamp a prepared camp, and we shall die in multitudes. But if we persevere, we shall take the mountain despite all the horrors there.

"Speak to your subchiefs. Tell them to seek volunteers—true volunteers, not coerced men—for a battle in which half of them will die. They will not be using their natural weapons. Those who enlist will be issued guns and shown how to use them."

Tyl stood up, smiling. "I have longed for the old days. Now they return."

Three thousand men of Tyl's monster tribe put aside their given weapons and took instruction in guns. Day and night Jim's small tribe spread out over the firing range, each man supervising one warrior at a time. When the gun had been mastered, the trainee was given the pistol or rifle and twenty rounds of ammunition and told to report back to the main camp. And *not to fire it* before the battle.

Var was kept busy relaying messages from the Master to Tyl and the subchiefs. The Weaponless pored over his map of the mountain and made notations for strategy and deployment. "We are shrews," he said mysteriously. "We must utilize shrew tactics. They know we're here, but they don't know exactly when or how we'll attack. They won't kill their hostages until they're sure they can't be used for bargaining purposes. We shall try to overwhelm them before they realize it. Even so, I do not expect to leave this campaign a happy man."

The only hostage Var knew of was Sol, the former master of the empire. Why should his welfare loom so important now? The Master could hardly care for competition again.

They were ready. The men were trained and deployed in a ring that went entirely around the mountain. Special troops guarded the subway and its connected tunnels, and no strangers were permitted anywhere in the vicinity. Wives and children had no place in this effort; they were removed to a camp of their own a day's walk distant, and married nonvolunteers guarded that region.

They were ready. But no attack was launched. Men chafed at the delay, eager to test their new weapons, eager to probe the dread defenses of the underworld. The mountain had a morbid fascination for them. They had guns and believed they could capture any fortress, but to take the mountain would be like conquering death itself!

Then, on the very worst day for such an effort, the Master put the troops in motion. He ignored Tyl's dismay and Var's perplexity. At the height of a blinding thunderstorm, they charged the mountain.

Var and Tyl stood beside the Nameless One, at his direction, each privately wondering what manner of man the leader had become. They watched the proceedings from an elevated and carefully protected blind. It was difficult to see anything in the rain, but they knew what to watch for.

"The lightning will knock out some of their television, temporarily," the Master explained. "It always does. The thunder will mask the noise of our firing. The rain will camouflage our physical advance and maybe suppress the effect of their flamethrowers. That, plus the masses of men involved, should do it."

The old campaigner was not so confused after all, Var realized. The mountaineers would assume that no attack could occur in rain and would not be ready.

The Master gave them field glasses—another salvaged device of the Ancients—and briefly demonstrated their use. With these they were able to see distant sections of the mountain as though they were close. The rain blurred the image some, but the effect was still striking.

Var watched a troop of men, bedraggled in the rain, follow a line toward the first projecting metal beams at the base of the mountain. The mountain was actually a morbid mass of gray, with stunted trees approaching the base and a few weeds sprouting here and there on its surface. Buzzards perched on the ugly projections, looking well fed. Even in the rain they waited, and surely they would feast today!

But there were paths up through the twisted metal, and these had been charted from a distance. The troops were prepared with cleats and hooks and would pass in minutes an obstruction that might take a naïve man half a day to navigate. Already the column he watched was beginning to splay, rushing for cover adjacent to the mountain.

Then the earth rose up and smote them down. Men were hurled through the air onto the bone-crushing rocks. Smoke erupted, obscuring the view.

"Mines," the Master said. "I was afraid of that."

"Mines," Tyl repeated, and Var was sure he was marking down one more thing to be well wary of in the future.

"They are buried explosives. We have no way to anticipate their location. Probably the weight of a single man is insufficient to trigger them, but when a full column passes—" He paused meaningfully. "The area should be safe for other troops now, because the mines have been expended."

The sound of more distant explosions suggested that other regions around the mountain were being made similarly safe. How did he know so much, Var wondered. The Master seemed to spend most of his time reading old tomes, yet it was as though he had traveled the world and plumbed its secrets.

A second wave of men charged through the steaming basin where the mines had exploded. They reached the foot of the mountain, taking cover as they had been drilled to do. But there seemed to be no fire from the defenders.

The warriors climbed through and under the twisted beams, following the pathways they knew. From this distance the column resembled a lashing snake, appearing and disappearing in partial cover. Then men ran out on the first plateau above.

And fire spurted from pipes rising from the ground.

Now Var believed. He fancied he could smell the scorching flesh as men spun about, smoking, and died.

Many died, but already more were coming up. They charged the pipes from the sides, for the fire flicked out in only one direction at a time. They fired bullets into the apertures, and those who retained clubs and staffs battered at the projections and bent them down, and finally the fires died. The rain continued, drenching everything.

"Your men are courageous and skilled," the Master said to Tyl.

Tyl was immune to the compliment. "On a sunny day, none would have survived. I know that now."

Then the return fire began. The thinned troops moved up the mountainside, but they were exposed to the concealed emplacements of the underworld—and the weapons mounted there were more than pistols.

"Machine guns," the Nameless One said, and flinched. "We cannot storm those. Sound the retreat."

But it was already too late. Few, very few, returned from the mountain.

When they totaled up the losses, known and presumed, they learned that almost a thousand men had perished in that lone engagement. Not one defender had been killed.

"Have we lost?" Var asked hesitantly in the privacy of the Master's command tent. He felt guilty for not finding and keeping properly secret a subterranean route into the mountain. All those brave men might have lived. . . .

"The first battle. Not the campaign. We will guard the territory we have cleared; they can't plant new mines or flamethrowers while we watch. Now we know where their machine guns are, too. We will lay siege. We will build catapults to bombard those nests. We will drop grenades on them. In time, the victory will be ours."

A warrior approached the entrance. "A paper, with writing," he said. "It was in a metal box that flew into our camp. It's addressed to you."

The Master accepted it. "Your literacy may have turned the course of battle," he said. Flattered, the man left.

Var knew that many of the women practiced reading, and some few of the men. Was it worthwhile after all?

The Master opened the paper and studied it. He smiled grimly. "We impressed them! They want to negotiate."

"They will yield without fighting?" Var didn't bother with all the awkward words, but that was his gist.

"Not exactly."

Var looked at him, again not comprehending. The Master read from the paper: "We propose, in the interests of avoiding senseless decimation of manpower and destruction of equipment, to settle the issue by contest of champions. Place: the mesa on top of Mount Muse, twelve miles south of Helicon. Date: August sixth, B-one-one-eight. Your choice of other terms of combat.

"Should our champion prevail, you will desist hostilities

and depart this region forever, and permit no other attack on Helicon. Should your champion prevail, we will surrender Helicon to you intact.

"Speak to the television set in the near hostel."

After a pause, the Master asked him: "How would you call it, Var?"

Var didn't know how to respond, so he didn't.

"Sound sensible to you? You think our champion could defeat theirs in single combat?"

Var had no doubt of the Master's ability to defeat any man the underworld could send against him, particularly if he specified weaponless combat. He nodded.

The Master drew out his map. "Here is the mountain he names. See how the contours crowd together?"

Var nodded again. But he realized that this was only part of the story.

"That means it is very steep. When I surveyed it, I saw that I could not climb it. Not rapidly, anyway. I am too heavy, too clumsy in that fashion. And there are boulders perched on the top."

Var visualized rocks crashing down, pushed by a fast climber onto the head of a slow climber. The Nameless One was matchless in combat, but rolled boulders could prevent him from ever reaching it. Perhaps the site had been selected to prevent him from participating, forcing the choice of a lesser man.

"Then—some other? We have many good warriors." Var said "we" though he knew he was not yet a part of the empire.

"It would be a test of climbing as well as fighting. And we have only two days to prepare, for today is August fourth by the underworld calendar."

"Tomorrow morning a climbing tournament!" Var said, knowing his speech had become incomprehensible in his excitement, but that the other would get his meaning.

The Weaponless smiled tiredly. "You don't suspect betrayal?"

He hadn't, until then. But he realized the nomads could still take the mountain by force, just as originally planned, if the mountain master did not honor the decision of the champions. So it seemed worthwhile.

The Weaponless fathomed his thinking. "All right. Tell Tyl to select fifty top warriors for a climbing tournament. To-

night I talk to the mountain; tomorrow we practice on
Mount Muse."

But he still did not look optimistic.

At dawn on the day of the tournament, Var stood at the
base of Mount Muse, waiting for sufficient light to climb.
Rather, for sufficient light for others to climb, for their eyes
were less sensitive in the dark than his own. He had known
he would be here the moment the Master agreed to hold
the tournament. Var, with his horny hands and hooflike
feet, and his years in the wilderness, was the most agile
climber in the camp, and he had chosen to compete. Since
he was not a member of the Master's empire, no one could
tell him no.

Tyl had seen him, though, and smiled, and said nothing.

And by noon Var was winner of the tournament.

"But he is yet a novice in the circle!" the Master protested, astonished by this development.

Tyl smiled. "Here are the next three winners of the climb.
Test him against them."

The Weaponless, worried, agreed. So Var, tired from his
morning effort but ready, faced the man who had reached
the top ten minutes after he had. Had it been the contest
of champions, on the mesa of Muse, Var would have had
ample time to cripple the man by dropping rocks on him.
That was the point of the climbing exercise: The best warrior in the empire would lose if he were too much slower
than the one the mountain master sent. But when it came
to the actual battle, the champion had to be more skilled
than the other too.

The second finisher was a staffer, nimble and lanky, who
had used his weapon cleverly to assist his climbing. Var entered the circle, running through in his mind the advice the
Master and Tyl had given him in the past: stick against staff.
The sticks were faster, the staff stronger. The sticks were
aggressive, the staff more passive. The sticks could launch a
dual offense, but it was hard to penetrate a good staff defense. And if the sticks did not break through early, eventually the staff would discover an opportunity and score.

The staffer was as well aware of the factors as was Var,
and more experienced. His advantage was time, and he ob-

viously meant to use it. He blocked conservatively, making
no mistakes, challenging Var to come to him.

Var obliged. He rapped at the weapon, not the man, creat-
ing a diversion while he searched for an opening. He feinted
at the head, at the feet, at the knuckles holding the staff,
until the man became a trifle slow in his responses, bored
with the harassment.

Then Var directed fierce blows at head and body simultaneously. The staff spun to counter both, but not quite
rapidly enough, because of the prior lulling byplay. The head
shot missed, but the body attack was successful. One rib at
least had been fractured.

As the man winced and brought his weapon over to catch
Var's exposed arm, Tyl stepped up to the circle. "First
blood!" he said. "Withdraw."

So Var had won. The advantage he had achieved would
normally have been sufficient to bring him eventual victory, and that was all he had needed to demonstrate. There
was no point in wearing himself out. His victory on that basis
would only militate against him in the real contest tomorrow.

The next man was a dagger. Var quailed inwardly when
he saw that, for the knives were as swift as the sticks, and
their contact more deadly. The sword and the club were
impressive weapons; but the dagger, competently wielded, was
more devastating in the confines of the circle.

But the knives had to be properly oriented. A thrust with
the flat of the blade was useless in many instances. And the
daggers were not apt instruments for blocking. Though more
effective offensively, they were less efficient overall than the
dual-purpose sticks.

Var had no choice. He had to fence with the blades,
paying first attention to his defense. If he could succeed in
making an opening for himself without sacrificing personal
protection, he could score. If not . . .

Now the dagger feinted at him, and Var had to react
conservatively, just as the staffer had against him. And the
result would be the same, with him the victim, unless he
could break the pattern.

But the dagger was tired. He was an older man, as old
as the Master. No doubt experience had made him a skilled
climber, but his age had made him pay for the effort. Not

much, not noticeably, except that Var did have a slight and increasing advantage in speed.

When he realized that, he knew he had won. With renewed confidence he beat back the blade thrusts, using his greater vigor to intercept every stroke and jar the hand that made it. Gradually he forced the man back, intercepting the thrusts sooner, and finally the hard-pressed dagger made an error, was bruised on the wrist and ruled the loser.

The third man was another sticker. "I am Hul," he said.

Var, fatigued from two circle encounters as well as the morning climb, knew then that he had lost his bid to be the empire's champion. For the sticker was one of the men Tyl had warned him about, one of the top fighters. Stick against stick Var could have no advantage except superior skill, and against this man he didn't have that.

Hul stood just outside the circle. "Var the Stick," he said, his voice resonant. "I have studied you and assessed you, and I can take you in the circle. Perhaps not next year, but today, yes. But you would bruise me before you went down, for you are strong and determined. This would make me less able tomorrow on the mesa and prejudice the case of the empire. Will you yield your place to me without combat?"

The request was reasonable. Hul was fresh, for he was young and strong too, and he had rested while Var fought. And if he had been tired he still could have won, for he was a master sticker. Tyl did not make errors about such rankings, for it was Tyl's business to rank the leading weapons of all the empire. And since Var was not of the empire he was answerable to no one but himself. Otherwise no subsidiary contest would have been necessary; the Master or Tyl could have selected the warrior with the best overall prospects and settled it. Var could step down with honor, having proven himself twice and now acting for the best interest of the empire.

But Var was not reasonable. The notion of losing the privilege of fighting for the Master, of being his champion —he thought he had won this in the climb and held it in the circle. Such a late sacrifice filled him with fury. "No!" he cried. It came out a growl. He would not give it up; it would have to be taken from him.

Unperturbed, Hul turned to Tyl. "Then, if the Weaponless permits, I shall yield to Var. One of us must conserve his strength; if we fight, neither will. He needs the respite; he *has* the spirit."

Tyl nodded, granting the Master's aquiescence. Var was to reflect on that act of Hul's many times in the years following and to learn something more each time he did so.

CHAPTER 9

Dawn again. This time he knew the best route, one that could cut as much as half an hour from his previous time. And he did not have to wait for any other man. But it was strenuous and dangerous, and he did not dare attempt it without suitable light. Natural light; if he used a flashlight, the other climber might spot him by it.

On the far side of Muse the mountain's champion would be ascending similarly. He would be naked, except perhaps for shoes, for the Master had stipulated that. Var was naked now. This was to ensure that no gun or other illicit weapon could be carried along secretly. The weapon the Master had specified was any of the recognized circle instruments: club, staff, stick, sword, dagger or star. Not rope or net or whip. Men of both groups would be watching from the fringes to see that neither climber was cheating on the terms in any other way.

Of course the fight on the mesa would not be very clear, because the watchers would be far below. But only the victor would descend alive, so there could be no doubt about that.

It was light enough. Var moved out, sticks anchored to his waist by a minimum harness. The chill of the morning pricked his skin. He was eager for the warming exercise—and, privately, to get away from the too-curious stares of the men at his exposed body. He knew he was not pretty.

He climbed. At first it was easy, for the slope was gentle and he avoided the crevices that might have trapped a foot in the dark. Then he struck the boulder-strewn wastes. This was where he gained time because of the superior route he had worked out. One man the day before had led him at this point, and he had been careful to note the particular path that man had happened on. He knew the mountain's champion would have to be a remarkable athlete to better Var's own time, for the other man would not have had this practice. Not recently, anyway. Of course he could have climbed Muse every day before the nomad siege began. That might be why such terms had been specified. Still, Var knew he was as fast as anyone here.

And he was sure that the other side was no better than his own. He had checked that out from the summit. There was nothing in the agreement to stop him from circling to that side in order to ascend more rapidly or intercept the other man. And he had verified that there was no secret, Ancient-built tunnel there either. So the terms were fair.

The last portion was the most difficult. Here the slope became so steep as to seem almost vertical. It wasn't; that was an illusion of perspective. But he did not peer down as he mounted it.

There were steplike terraces and crevices, ranging from mere lines in the wall to platforms several feet wide. Here Var's stubby, calloused fingers and hard bare toes were important assets, for he could find lodging on a minimum basis. Up, across and around he went, traversing the open face of the mountain, keeping a nervous eye for falling rocks. If the other champion *had* somehow reached the summit first . . .

But Var triumphed. No boulders were loosed on him, and when he poked his head over the brim, alert for attack, he found it bare.

Now it would be up to his ability with the sticks.

He trotted to the far side of the little mesa. The platform was only about ten paces in diameter, twice that of the battle circle, but hardly seeming so because of the frightening drop-off all around. He peered over.

The underworld's warrior was climbing. Var observed his bare back, his round head, his moving limbs, but was unable to make out much detail. He judged the man to be about five minutes from the summit. That was a kind of relief, for it meant that Var's selection as the empire champion had been valid. The slower warriors would have reached the top too late. Particularly Hul. What good would Hul's skill and courage have done him if his head were bashed in while he still climbed?

Var glanced at the available stones. Some were small, suitable for throwing. Some were good for accurate dropping. A few were large enough for rolling—and woe betide what lay in their crushing paths!

He picked up a throwing rock, nestling it in his palm. His grip was awkward, but he could throw well enough. He peered down at the warrior. The man was clinging to the rim of the shelf, inching from one narrow step to another. He was helpless; if he tried to dodge a falling object, he would fall himself. And he wasn't even looking up. It was as though the notion of such a premature attack had not occurred to him.

Var set the stone down, disgusted with himself for being tempted, and recrossed the mesa. The Master had invariably stressed the importance of honor outside the circle, until this present adventure. Within the circle there was no law at all except death and victory; outside there was no victory without honor. This plateau was the effective circle. The men of the underworld might not practice honor in the fashion of the nomads, but this one circumscribed case was plainly an exception. He had to let the warrior enter before making any hostile move.

Var was sitting crosslegged at his own side of the mesa as the other warrior clambered to the level section. The first thing Var saw was the sticks slung from a neck loop. He was matched against his own weapon!

The second thing he saw was that the other warrior was small—in fact, diminutive to the point of dwarfism. His head would barely reach Var's shoulder, and Var, though large, was no giant.

The third thing he did not see. The naked warrior was either castrate—

Or female.

"I am ready," the mountain champion said, grasping the two sticks and dropping the harness over the edge.

It was a girl, definitely. Her voice was high, sweet. She had thick black hair cut short beneath the ears, delicate facial features, a lithe slender body, and tightly bound sandals on her feet. She could not be more than nine years old. Half his own age, by the Master's reckoning.

There could be no mistake. She was here, she was armed, she was not shy or surprised. The underworld had sent a child to represent its interests.

Why? Surely they were not depending on some chivalrous dispensation to give the little girl the technical victory? Not when the fate of mountain and empire was at stake. Not when a thousand men had died already in the larger combat. Yet if they *wanted* to lose, it had hardly been necessary to make such an elaborate arrangement, or to sacrifice a child.

Var got up and disposed of his own harness, mainly to have something to do while he tried to think. It occurred to him that he should be embarrassed to be naked in the presence of a girl, but his social conditioning dated only from his contact with civilization and was not universally deep. The codes of honor were more immediate than personal modesty. And this was not a woman but a child. Except for her peeking cleft, she could be a young boy. Her hair was no longer, her chest no more developed.

He thought irrelevantly of Sola.

He came to meet the child cautiously, doubting that she could wield the full-sized sticks adequately.

Her slender arms moved rapidly. Her two sticks countered his own with expertise. She did know what she was doing.

So they fought. Var had size and strength, but the child had speed and skill. The match, astonishingly, was even.

Gradually Var realized that this strange situation was not at all a game. He had been prepared to battle a vicious man to the death and had trouble coping with a female child. Yet if he did not defeat her (he could not now bring himself to think "kill"), he would be defeated himself, and the Master's cause would be lost.

Better to do it quickly. He attacked with fury, using his brute strength to beat the girl back toward the brink. She stepped back, and back again, but could not do so indefinitely. Stick met stick, no blow landing on flesh directly, but Var applied pressure as he had done with the dagger the day before, and improved his position.

She was two steps from the edge, then one. Then she spun about without seeming to look, knocked one of his sticks up, ducked under it, scooted past him, and caught his wrist with a backhand swing that completely surprised him.

Var laughed incredulously as one of his sticks flew from his numbed hand and rattled down the mountainside. The maneuver had been so swiftly and neatly executed that he had not had the chance to defend against it. Now, half-disarmed, he was virtually lost. One stick could not prevail against two.

His inexperience in the circle had after all cost him the match. Hul would not have been caught so simply, and certainly not Tyl. Yet who would have expected such skill from a mere child?

Var waited for the attack that had to come. He was doomed, but he would not give up. Perhaps a lunge would catch her unaware in turn, or maybe he could throw them both off the mesa, making the battle a tie in mutual death.

She looked at him a moment. Then, casually, she tossed one of her own sticks after his—over the brink.

Dumfounded, Var saw it clatter out of play. She could have tapped him on the skull in that moment without opposition, but she kept her distance. "You—"

"So you owe me one," she said. "Fair fight." And she came at him with the single stick.

Var had to fight, but he was shaken. She had disarmed herself to make the match even again. When she could have had easy victory. He had never imagined such a thing in the circle.

There was no doubt that she meant business, however. She pressed him hard with her half-weapon and scored repeatedly on his unarmed side. It was a strange off-balance contest, requiring unusual contortions and reflexes to compensate for the missing stick, and the finesse of the dual weapons was largely gone.

Thus clumsily they fought. And Var, because the reduction of finesse brought her skill closer to his own level without correspondingly upgrading her strength, gradually gained the initiative. But he pursued it with restraint, for he did not need a second such lesson as the one that had cost him one stick. The child was most dangerous when she seemed most beleaguered.

And he still wasn't certain what her sacrifice of her own stick meant. Surely she could not have been so confident of victory that she disarmed herself for the joy of enhanced competition! And surely she could not desire to *lose*. . . .

Var had not survived his childhood in the badlands without being alert to the dangers of the unknown. Not all unknowns were physical.

She was tiring, and he slacked off some more, supercautious. The height of the sun showed they had been at it for some three hours, and now the afternoon was passing.

But how would it end, with their life-and-death battle reduced to mere sparring? Only one of them could descend the mountainside. Only one team could prevail. Delay could not change that harsh reality.

If the contest did not end soon, the victor would not have enough time remaining before dusk to make a safe descent. Mount Muse was challenging at any time and seemed impossible in the dark.

It did not end soon. The battle had become a mockery, for neither person was really trying to win. Not immediately, anyway. Both were holding back, conserving strength, waiting for some more crucial move by the other—a move that did not come. Stick still beat against stick, but the force was perfunctory, the motions routine.

Dusk did come. The girl stepped back, dropping her weapon. "We shouldn't fight at night," she said.

Var lowered his own weapon, agreeing, but alert for betrayal.

She walked to the edge, leaving her stick behind. "Don't look," she said. She squatted.

Var realized that she had to urinate. But if he turned his back she could run up behind him, push. . . . Still, if he could not trust her during this period of truce, he had had no business agreeing to it. And there had been that matter of the extra stick. Her codes were different than his, but they seemed consistent. He faced outward and relieved his own bladder into the gloom below.

Their toilets done, the two returned to the center of the plateau. Darkness filled the landscape like a great ocean, but their island remained clear. And lonely.

"I'm hungry," she said.

So was he. But there was nothing to eat. All concerned had assumed that the battle would be of short duration, so no provision for a prolonged stay had been made. Perhaps this had been intentional: If the champions did not fight with sufficient vigor, thirst and hunger would prompt them.

"You don't talk much, do you?" she said.

"I don't talk well," Var explained. The mangled syllables conveyed the message more clearly than the language did.

Oddly, she smiled, a flash of white in shadow. "My father doesn't talk at all. He got hurt in the throat years ago.

Before I can remember. But I understand him well enough."

Var just nodded.

"Why don't you take that side, and I'll take this side, and we'll sleep," she said, gesturing. "Tomorrow we'll finish this."

He agreed. He took his stick and skuffed it across the center of the plateau, making a line that divided the area in halves. He lay down in his territory.

The girl sat up for a while, looking very small. "What's your name?"

"Var."

"Who?"

"Var."

"I don't see any bad scar on your throat. Why can't you talk?"

Var tried to figure out a simple way to answer that, but failed.

"What's it like, outside?" she asked.

He realized that he did not need to reply sensibly to her questions. She was more interested in talking than in listening.

"It's cold," she said.

Var hadn't thought about it, but she was right. A hard chill was settling on the mesa, and they were both naked and without sleeping bags. He could endure it, of course; he had slept exposed many times in his youth. But she was smaller than he and thinner, and her skin was soft.

In fact, the cold would be more than an inconvenience to her. She could die from exposure. Already her hunched hairless torso was shaking so violently he felt the tremors in the ground.

Var sat up. "That favor I owe you, for the stick—" he called.

Her head turned toward him. He could see the motion, but nothing else in the fading light. "I don't understand."

"For the stick—my return favor." He tried to enunciate clearly.

"Stick," she said. "Favor." She was beginning to pick up his clumsy words, but not his meaning. Her teeth chattered as she spoke.

"The warmth of my body, tonight."

"Warm? Night?" She remained perplexed.

Var got up abruptly and crossed over to her. He lay down

on his side, took hold of her, and pulled her to him. "Sleep —warm," he said as clearly as he could.

For a moment her body was tense, and her hands flew to his neck in a gesture he recognized from demonstrations the Nameless One had made. *She knew weaponless combat!* Then she relaxed.

"You mean to share warmth! Thank you, Var!" And she turned about, curled up and lay with her shivering back nestled against his front, his arms and legs falling about her. His chin, sprouting its sparse beard, came to nestle in her fluffy hair. His forearm settled on her folded thigh, his hand clasped her knee to gain the purchase necessary to keep them close together.

Var remembered the first time he had held a woman, not so many months before. But of course this was not the same. Sola had been buxom and hot, while this child was bony and cold. And the relationship was entirely different. Yet he found this chaste camaraderie against the cold to be as meaningful as that earlier sexual connection. To stand even on the favors—that was part of the circle code, as he understood it, and there was no shame in it.

Yet in the morning they would do battle again.

"Who are you?" he asked now. For once the words came out succinctly.

"Soli. My father is Sol of All Weapons."

Sol of All Weapons! The former master of the empire, and the man who had built it up from nothing. No wonder she was so proficient!

Then a terrible thought struck him. "Your mother, who is your mother?"

"Oh, my mother knows even more about fighting than Sol does, but she does it without weapons. She's very small, hardly bigger than I am, and I'm not full grown, but any man who comes at her lands on his head!" She tittered. "It's funny."

Relief, until something else occurred to him. "She—your mother—brown curly hair, very good figure, smock—"

"Yes, that's her! But how could you know? She's never been out of the underworld, not since I've been there."

Once again Var found himself at a loss to explain. Certainly he did not want to tell her he had tried to kill her mother.

"Of course Sosa isn't my natural mother," Soli remarked.

"I was born outside. My father brought me in when I was small."

Var's earlier shock returned. "You—you're Sola's dead daughter?"

"Well, we're not really dead in the underworld. We just let the nomads think that, because—I don't know exactly why. Sol was married to Sola outside, though, and I'm their child. They say Sola married the Nameless One after that."

"Yes. But she kept her name."

"Sosa kept her name, too. That's funny."

But Var was remembering Sola's charge to him: *"Kill the man who harms my child."*

Var the Stick was that man, for he was pledged to save the empire by killing the mountain's champion.

CHAPTER 10

Var woke several times in the night, beset by the chill of this height. A wind came up, wringing the precious warmth from his back. Only in front, where he touched Soli, was he warm. He could have survived alone, but it was better this way.

Every so often the girl stirred, but when her limbs stretched out and met the cold, they contracted again quickly. Even so, her hands were icy. Had she slept by herself, she would hardly have been able to wield a stick in the morning. Var put his coarse hand over her fine one, shielding it.

Dawn finally came. They stood up shivering and jumped vigorously to restore circulation; they attended to natural calls again, but it was some time before they both felt better. Fog shrouded the plateau, making the drop-off unreal, the sky dismal.

"What's that?" Soli inquired, pointing.

Once more, Var was at a loss to answer. He knew what it was, but not what women called it.

"My father, Sol, doesn't have one," she said.

Var knew she was mistaken, for had that been the case she herself would never have been born.

"I'm hungry," she said. "And thirsty too."

So was Var, but they were no closer to a solution to that problem than they had been the night before. They had to fight. The winner would descend and feast as royally as he or she wished. The other would not need food again, ever. He looked at the two singlesticks lying across the center-line. A pair—but one his, the other hers.

She saw his glance. "Do we have to fight?"

Var never seemed to be able to answer her questions. On

70

the one hand he represented the empire; on the other, he had his oath to Sola to uphold. He shrugged.

"It's foggy," she said wistfully. "Nobody can see us."

Meaning that they should not fight without witnesses? Well, it would do for an excuse. The mist showed no sign of dissipating, and no sound rose from its depths. The world was a whiteness, as was their contest.

"Why don't we go down and get some food?" she asked. "And come back before they see us."

The simplicity and directness of her mind were astonishing! Yet, why not? He was glad to have a pretext to postpone hostilities, since he could not see his way clear either to winning or losing.

"Truce—until the fog lifts?" he asked.

"Truce—until the fog lifts. That time I understood you very well."

And Var was pleased.

They descended on Var's side of the mountain, after retrieving the stick harnesses. The third and fourth sticks themselves had bounced and rolled and been lost entirely, but the harnesses had stayed where they fell. Soli had feared that the underworld had ways to spot anyone who traversed her own slope of Mt. Muse. "Television pickups— can't tell where they're hidden."

"You mean sets are just sitting around outside?" Var knew what television was; he had seen the strange silent pictures on the boxes in hostels.

"Sets, outside," she repeated, interpreting. "No, silly. Pickups—little boxes like eyes set into stones and things, operated by remote control."

Var let the subject drop. He had never seen a stone with an eye in it, but there had been stranger things in the badlands.

The fog was even thicker at the base. They held hands and sneaked up to the Master's camp. Then Var hesitated. "They'll know me," he whispered.

"Oh." She was taken aback. "Could I go in then?"

"You don't know the layout."

"I'm *hungry!*" she wailed.

"Shh." He jerked her back out of hearing range. A warrior sentry could come on them at any time.

"Tell me the layout," she whispered desperately. "I'll go in and steal some food for us."

"Stealing isn't honest!"

"It's all right in war. From an enemy camp."

"But that's *my* camp!"

"Oh." She thought a moment. "I could still go. And ask for some. They don't know me."

"Without any clothes?"

"But I'm *hungry!*"

Var was getting disgusted and didn't answer. His own hunger became intense.

She began to cry.

"Here," Var said, feeling painfully guilty. "The hostel has clothes."

They ran to the hostel, one mile. Before Var could protest, Soli handed him her harness and stick and walked inside. She emerged a few minutes later wearing a junior smock and a hair ribbon and new sandals, looking clean and fresh.

"You're lucky no one was there!" Var said, exasperated.

"Someone *was* there. Somebody's wife, waiting to meet her warrior. I guess they're keeping the women out of your main camp. She jumped a mile when I walked in. I told her I was lost, and she helped me."

So neatly accomplished! He would never have thought of that, or had the nerve to do it. Was she bold or naïve?

"Here," she said. She handed him a bundle of clothing.

Dressed, they reappraised the main camp. It occurred to Var that there should have been food at the hostel, but then he remembered that the nomads cleaned it out regularly. It took a lot of food to feed an armed camp, and the hostel food was superior to the empire mess. Otherwise they might have solved their problem readily. Their *food* problem.

"I'll have to go to the main tent," she said. Var agreed, hunger making him urgent, now that their nakedness had been abated. "I'll pretend I'm somebody's daughter and that I'm bringing food out to my family."

Var was fearful of this audacity but could offer nothing better. "Be careful," he said.

He lurked in the forest near the tent, not daring to move for fear she would not be able to find him again. She disappeared into the mist.

Then he remembered what her plan should have jogged into his head before: The entire camp was not only masculine, it was on a recognition-only basis. No stranger could pass the guards, particularly not a female child.

And it was too late to stop her.

Soli moved toward the huge tent, fascinated by its tenuous configuration though her heart beat nervously. She would have felt more confident with a pair of sticks but had left them with Var because children—especially girl children—did not carry weapons here.

A guard stood at the tent entrance. She tried to brush past him as if she belonged, but his staff came down to bar her immediately. "Who are you?" he demanded.

She knew better than to give her real name. Hastily she invented one: "I'm Sami. My father is tired. I have to fetch some food for—"

"No Sam in this camp, girl. I'd know a strange name like that for sure. What game are you playing?"

"Sam the Sword. He just arrived. He—"

"You're lying, child. No warrior brings his family into *this* camp. I'm taking you to the Master." He nudged her with the staff.

No one else was in sight at the moment. Soli vaulted the pole, shot spoked fingers at his eyeballs, and when his head jerked back in the warrior's reflex she sliced him across the throat with the rigid side of her hand. She clipped him again as he gasped for breath, and he collapsed silently.

He was too heavy for her to move, so she left him there and stepped inside, straightening her rumpled smock and retying her hair. She could still get the food if she acted quickly enough.

But the morning mess was over, and she did not dare pester the cook directly.

"Kol has been attacked!" someone shouted back at the entrance. "Search the grounds!"

Oh—oh. She hadn't gotten out in time. But her hunger still drove her. She would have to make up for her vulnerability by sheer audacity, as Sosa put it. Sosa knew how to make the best of bad situations.

She retreated to just shy of the entrance, knowing what must happen there.

Warriors rushed up, hauled the unconscious Kol to his feet, exclaiming: "Didn't see it happen." "Clubbed in the throat." "Spread a net—he can't have gotten far."

Then a huge man came. Soli recognized him at once: the Nameless One, master of the enemy empire. He moved like a rolling machine, shaking the ground with the force of his

tread, and he was ugly. His voice was almost as bad as
Var's.

"That was a weaponless attack. The mountain has sent a
spy."

Soli didn't wait for more. She ran out of the tent and
threw herself at the monster, arms outstretched.

Surprised, he caught her by the shoulders and lifted her
high, his strength appalling. "What have we here?"

"Sir!" she cried. "Help me! A man is chasing me!"

"A child!" he said. "A girl child. What family?"

"No family. I'm an orphan. I came here for food—"

The Master set her down, but one hand gripped her thin
shoulder with viselike power. "The hand that struck Kor's
neck would have been about the size of your hand, child.
I saw the mark. You are a stranger, and I know the ways
of the mountain. You—"

She reacted even before she fully comprehended his im-
port. Her pointed knuckles rammed into his cloak, aiming
for the solar plexus as she twisted away.

It was like hitting a wall. His belly was made of steel.

"Try again, little spy," he said, laughing.

She tried again. Her knee came up to ram hard into his
crotch, and one hand struck at his neck.

The Nameless One just stood there chuckling. His grip on
her shoulder never loosened. With his free hand he tore open
his own cloak.

His torso was a grotesque mass of muscle that did not
flex properly with his breathing. His neck was solid gristle.

"Child, I know your leader's tricks. What are you doing
here? Our contest was supposed to be settled by combat of
champions on the plateau."

"Sir, I—I thought he was attacking me. He moved his
shaft—" She searched for a suitable story. "I'm from Tribe
Pan." That was Sosa's tribe, before she came to the mountain; it trained its women in weaponless combat. "I ran away.
All I wanted was food."

"Tribe Pan." He pondered. Something strangely soft crossed
his brutal face. "Come with me." He let go of her and
marched out of the crowd.

No other warrior spoke. She knew better than to attempt
any break now. Docilely, she followed the Weaponless.

He entered a large private tent. There was food there;
her empty stomach ached from its aroma.

"You are hungry—eat," he said, setting a bowl of porridge and a cup of milk before her.

Eagerly she reached for both, then fathomed the trap. Nomad table manners differed from underworld practice. Her every mannerism would betray her origin. In fact, she wasn't sure the nomads used utensils at all.

She plunged one fist into the porridge and brought up a dripping gob. She smeared this into her mouth, wincing at its heat. She ignored the milk.

The Nameless One did not comment.

"I'm thirsty," she said after a bit.

Wordlessly he brought her a winebag.

She put the nozzle to her mouth and sucked. She gagged. It was some bitter, bubbling concoction. "That isn't water!" she cried, her anguish real.

"At Pan they have neither hostels nor home brew?" he inquired.

Then she realized that she had overdone it. Most nomads *would* know the civilized mode of eating, for the hostels had plates and forks and spoons and cups. And the truly uncivilized tribes must drink brew.

Soli began to cry, sensing beneath this brute visage a gentle personality. It was her only recourse.

He brought her water.

"It doesn't make sense," he said as she drank. "Bob would not send an unversed child into the enemy heartland. That would be stupid, particularly at this time."

Soli wondered how he had learned her chief's name. Oh, they had communicated, to arrange the fight on Muse plateau.

"Yet no ordinary child would know weaponless combat," he continued.

She realized that somehow her very mistakes had helped put him off. "Can I take some back to my friend?" she asked, remembering Var.

The Nameless One looked as though he were about to ask a question, then exploded into laughter. "Take all you can carry, you gamin! May your friend feast for many days and emerge from his orgy a happier man than I!"

"I really do have a friend," she said, nettled at his tone. She realized that he was mocking her, supposing that she wanted it all for herself.

He brought a bag and tossed assorted solids into it as well as two wineskins. "Take this and get out of my camp, child.

Far out. Go back to Pan—they produce good women, even the barren ones. *Especially* those. We're at war here, and it isn't safe for you, even with your defensive skills."

She slung the heavy sack over her shoulder and went to the exit.

"Girl!" he called suddenly, and she jumped, afraid he had seen through her after all. Bob, the master of Helicon, was like that; he would toy with a person, seeming to agree, then take him down unexpectedly and savagely. "If you ever grow tired of wandering, seek me out again. I would take you for my daughter."

She understood with relief that this was a fundamental compliment. And she liked this enormous, terrible man. "Thank you," she said. "Maybe some day you'll meet my real father. I think you would like each other."

"You were not an orphan long, then," he murmured, chuckling again. He was horribly intelligent under that muscle. "Who is your father?"

Suddenly she remembered that the two men *had* met, for the Nameless One had taken the empire and her true mother from her father. She dared not give Sol's name now, for the men had to be mortal enemies.

"Thank you," she said quickly, pretending not to have heard him. "Good-bye, sir." And she ducked out of the tent.

He let her go. No hue and cry followed, and no secret tracker either.

CHAPTER 11

Var's body felt weak as he saw Soli come out of the thinning mist alone. No one was following her; he let her pass him and waited just to be sure.

Yet he had heard the outcry and seen the men rushing to the main tent. Its entrance was hidden from him in the fog, but he had thought he heard her voice and the Master's. Something had happened, and he had been powerless to act or even to know. He had had to wait, nervously clasping and unclasping his rough fingers about the two sticks, his and hers. If she were prisoner, what would happen next?

She circled back silently, searching for him. Somehow she had talked her way out of it, if he had not imagined the whole thing, converting other voices to those he knew. "Here," he whispered. She ran at him and shoved a heavy bag into his hands. Together they hurried away from the camp. He knew no one would trace them in this fog, and the terrain was too rough for their traces to show later.

At the base of Muse they paused while he fished in the sack for the food he smelled. He found a wineskin and gulped greedily, squirting it into his mouth. It was good, sturdy nomad beer, the kind of beverage the crazies never provided. Then he got hold of a loaf of dark bread and gnawed on it as they climbed.

The edge of his hunger assuaged, Var worried about the fog. If it let up before they reached the top, their secret would be out. Then what would they do?

But it held. With mutual relief they flopped on the mesa, panting. They emptied the bag on the ground and feasted.

There was bread, of course. There was roasted meat. There were baked potatoes. There were apples and nuts and even some crazy chocolate. One wineskin held milk, the other the beer.

"How," Var demanded around a mouthful, "did you get all this?"

Soli, not really hungry because of the porridge she had already had, experimented again with the beer. She had never had any before today, and it intrigued her by its very foulness. "I asked the Nameless One for it."

Var choked, spewing potato crumbs out wastefully. "How—why—?"

She gulped down another abrasive mouthful of beer, repressing its determined urge to come up again, and told him the story. "And I wish they weren't enemies," she finished. "Sol and the Nameless One—they would like each other otherwise. Your Master is sort of nice, even though he's terrible."

"Yes," Var murmured, thinking of his own intimate five-year experience with the man. "But they aren't really enemies. The Master told me once. They were friends, but they had to fight for some reason. Sol gave the Weaponless his wife, with his bracelet and all. Because she didn't want to die, and she didn't love Sol anyway."

She looked confused through most of that speech, having to puzzle out his inflections, but she reacted immediately to the last of it. "She did too love him!" she flared. "She was my mother!"

He backed away from that aspect, disturbed. "She's a good woman," he said after a moment. That seemed to mollify Soli, though Var was thinking of the journey he had made with Sola. He could see the resemblance now, between mother and daughter. But could Sola have loved *anyone* to have done what she did? Jumping from man to man and putting her body to secret service for Var himself? Surely the Master knew—she had *said* he knew—yet he allowed it. How could such a thing be explained?

And once more he came up against the problem of his oath to Sola: to kill the man who harmed her child. What sort of a woman Sola was or why she should be so concerned *now* for a child she deserted *then*—these things had no mitigating relevance. He had sworn. How could he fight Soli now?

"Friends," Soli said forlornly. "I could have told him . . ." She gulped more beer and let out a nomadlike belch.

"Var, if we fight and I kill you then the Weaponless will

go away, and Sol will never see him. Again." She began to cry once more.

"We can't fight," Var said, relieved to make it official.

The fog lifted.

"They can see us!" Soli cried, jumping up. This was not true, for the ground remained shrouded, but the nether mists were thinning too. "They'll know. The sticks!" And she fell down again.

"What's the matter?" Var asked, scrambling to help her.

She rolled her head. "I feel funny." Then she vomited.

"The beer!" Var said, angry with himself for not thinking what it would do to her. He had been sick himself the first time he had been exposed to it. "You must have drunk a quart while we talked."

But the bag was not down nearly that much. Soli just hung on him and heaved.

Var grabbed a soft sugared roll and sponged off her face and front with it. "Soli, you can't be sick now. They're watching, your people and mine. If we don't fight—"

"Where's my stick?" she cried hysterically. "I'll bash your humpy head in. Leave me alone!" She tried another heave, but nothing came up.

Var held her erect, not knowing what else to do. He was afraid that if he let her go she would either collapse on the ground or stumble over the brink. Either way, it wouldn't be much of a show, and the watchers on either side would become suspicious.

A show! To the distant spectators, it must appear that the two were in a terminal struggle, staggering about the mesa after an all-night combat. This was the fight!

"Wanna sleep," Soli mumbled. "Lie down. Sick. Keep the cold off me, Var, there's a good nomad. . . ." Her knees folded.

Var hooked his arms under her shoulders and held her up. "We can't sleep. Not while they're watching."

"I don't care. Let me go." She lapsed into sobbing again.

Var had to set her down.

"It's that beer, isn't it," she said, suddenly wide awake. "I'm drunk. They never let me have any. Sol and Sosa. Awful stuff. Hold me, Var. I feel all weak. I'm frightened."

Var decided that any further show of battle was hopeless. He lay down and put his arms about her, and she cried and cried.

After a time she regained self-control. "What'll we do, Var?"

He didn't know.

"Could we both go home and say it didn't work?" she asked plaintively. Then, before he could answer, she did: "No. Bob would kill me as a traitor. And the war would go on."

They sat side by side and looked out over the world.

"Why don't we tell them somebody *won?*" she asked suddenly. "Then it'll be settled."

Var was dubious, but as he considered it the proposal seemed sound. "Who wins?"

"We'll have to choose. If I win, you nomads will go away. If you win, they'll take over the underworld. Which is better?"

"There'll be a lot of killing if we go down there," he said. "Maybe your—maybe Sol and Sosa."

"No," she said. "Not if Helicon surrenders. And you said they were friends, Sol and the Nameless One. They could be together again. And I could meet Sola, my true mother." Then, after a moment: "She couldn't be better than Sosa, though."

He thought about that, and it seemed reasonable. "I win, then?"

"You win, Var." She gave him a wan smile and reached for the bread.

"But what about you?"

"I'll hide. You tell them I'm dead."

"But Sol—"

"After it's over, I'll find Sol and tell him I'm not dead. By then it won't make any difference."

Var still felt uneasy, but Soli seemed so certain that he couldn't protest. "Go *now,*" she urged. "Tell him it was a hard battle and you fell down too, but you finally won."

"But I'm unmarked!"

She giggled. "Look at your arm."

He looked at both arms. His right was clean, but his left, the weaponless one, was laced with bruises. She had been scoring, that serious part of the fight. Soli herself was almost without blemish.

"I could bash you in the face a couple of times," she said mischievously. "To make it look better." She tried to sup-

press a titter and failed. "I think I said that wrong. The fight,
I mean. It isn't that ugly. Your face, I mean."

Var left her there and began his descent. She would
play dead until dusk, then make her way down the safest
route as well as she could. He worried, but she told him
that she knew the way and anyhow would have plenty of
time to be careful. Certainly he couldn't wait for her. "I'll
start down before it's all the way dark," she said. "So I'll
be past the killer slope before I can't see any more."

He halted a few feet down and called up to her: "If anything happens, where can I find you?" He could not get rid
of his morbid concern.

"Near the hostel," she called back. "Hurry up. I mean
down."

He obliged, not avoiding abrasions since they would make
his supposed fight to the death seem more authentic. He
would be telling a lie, but at least he was doing the right
thing, and he had also preserved his oath. He had learned
the final lesson the Master had taught him.

"Var! Va-a-ar!" Soli was calling him, her dark head poked
over the edge.

"What?"

"Your clothing!"

He had forgotten! He was wearing the stolen clothing.
If he returned in that, everything would be exposed, ironi-
cally.

Embarrassed, he returned to the mesa and stripped to the
skin. The material would help keep her warm anyway.

There was jubilation that night at the Master's base camp,
and Var was feted in a manner he was wholly unaccustomed
to. He had to eat prodigiously, not daring to admit he
was not hungry. For the first time the women of the neighboring camp, suspiciously quick to appear after word of the
victory had spread, found him attractive. But all he could
think of was little Soli struggling down the treacherous cliffs
in the dark, carrying her bundle of food and clothing. If
she fell their ruse would become reality. . . .

The warriors assumed that he had fought a male sticker,
and Var chose to avoid clarification of the matter. "I killed,"
he said, and stopped there. He fended off male congratula-

tions and female attentions until finally Tyl saw the way of it and found him a private tent for the night.

In the morning the Master went to the hostel to talk to the television set, taking Var along. The Master had not questioned him and seemed apprehensive. "If Bob pulls a double-cross, this is when it will happen," he muttered. "He is not the type to yield readily, ever."

Soli's own assessment of the underworld master seemed to concur. That must be a devil of a man, Var thought.

They entered the elegant cylindrical building, with its racks of clothing and sanitary facilities and its several machineries, and the Master turned on the set. As it warmed up, Var realized that once again they had blundered safely past disaster, for if that set had been on when Soli came, the underworld would have known what was happening.

The picture that came on was not the random, vapid collection of costumed posturings Var had observed from time to time before. Nor was it silent. It was a room, not like the hostel room, but certainly the work of crazy machines. It was square, with diagrams on the opposite wall and air vents and a ponderous metal desk in the center. In fact, it was rather like a room in a building such as he had prowled through in the badlands. But clean and new, not filthy and ancient.

A man sat in a padded, bendable chair behind the desk. He was old, older than the Master, at least thirty and possibly more. Var did not know how long a man could live if he suffered no mishap in the circle. Perhaps even as long as forty years. This one had sparse gray-brown hair (actually, the picture was colorless, but that was the way it looked) and stern lines in his face.

"Hello, Bob," the Master said grimly.

"Hello again, Sos. What's the word?" The man's tones were brisk, assured, and he moved his long thin arm as though directing subordinates. A leader of men, yes. Var did not like him.

"Your champion did not return?"

The man merely stared coldly at him.

"This is Var the Stick, our champion," the Master said. "He informs me that he killed your champion on the mesa of Muse yesterday."

"Impossible. Surely you realize no lesser man than yourself could have defeated Sol of All Weapons in honest combat."

The Master seemed stricken. "Sol! You sent Sol?"

"Ask your supposed champion," Bob said.

The Master turned slowly to Var. "Sol would not have gone. But if he had——"

"No," Var said. "It wasn't Sol." He didn't understand why the underworld leader should play such a game.

"Perhaps, then, his mate, if the term is not unkindly euphemistic," Bob said, his glance conveying a peculiar intensity. "She of the deadly hands and barren womb."

"No!" Var cried, knowing now that he was being baited, but reacting to it anyway. The Master, astonishingly, was sweating. It was as though the real battle was taking place here, rather than on the mesa. A strange contest of deadly words and savage implications. And Bob was winning it.

Bob looked at his fingernails during the pause. "Who, then?"

Var spoke quietly. "His daughter. Soli. She had sticks."

The Master opened his mouth but did not speak. He stared at Var as though pierced by a bullet.

"I apologize," Bob said smoothly. "Var was there, after all. He did kill our designated champion. Her parents were too wary to cooperate, so are in our bad graces; but she was, shall we say, cooperatively naïve. Of course she was only eight years old—eight and a half or better, technically—and I think we'll have to delay further action on this matter in favor of a rematch. . . ."

Var realized that the man's overelaborate words signified his intent to renege. But the Master was not protesting. The Master continued to stare dumbly at Var.

There was another wait. "You . . . killed . . . Soli?" the Master said at last, so hoarsely as to be hardly comprehensible.

Var did not dare tell the full truth here before the underworld leader. "Yes."

The Master's whole body shook as though he were cold. Var could not understand what was the matter. Soli was no relation to him; the Master had not even known her when she begged food from him. True, it was unkind to kill a girl but he had had to meet the mountain's champion, in whatever guise. Had it been a mutant lizard, he still would have fought. Why was the Master so upset now, and why was Bob looking so smug? They were acting as though he had *lost* the battle.

"So I was correct about her," Bob said. "Sol never let on. But obviously—"

"Var the Stick," the Master said formally, his voice quivering with emotion. "The friendship between us is ended. Where we meet next, there is the circle. No terms but death. In deference to your ignorance and to what is past, I give you one day and one night to flee. Tomorrow I come for you."

Then he whirled and smote the television set with his massive fist. The glass on the face of it shattered and the box toppled over. "And after that, *you!*" he shouted at the dead machine. "Not one chamber will escape the flame-thrower, and you shall roast on the pyre, alive!"

Var had never seen such fury in any man. He understood none of it, except that the Master intended to kill both him and the underworld leader. His friend had lost his sanity.

Var fled from the hostel and kept on running, confused and ashamed and afraid.

CHAPTER 12

"Var."

He whirled, grabbing for his new set of sticks. Then he relaxed. "Soli!"

"I saw you run from the hostel. So I came too. Var, what happened?"

"The Master——" Var was stopped by an unmanly misery. "He——"

"Wasn't he happy that you won?"

"The——Bob reneged."

"Oh." She took his hand solicitously. "So it was for nothing. No wonder the Weaponless is mad. But that isn't your fault, is it?"

"He says he'll kill me."

"Kill you? The Nameless One? Why?"

"I don't know." It was as though she were the inquiring adult, he the child.

"But he's nice. Underneath. He wouldn't do that. Not just because it didn't work."

Var shrugged. He had seen the Master run amuck. He believed.

"What are you going to do, Var?"

"Leave. He's giving me a day and a night."

"But what will *I* do? I can't go back to the mountain now. Bob would kill me, and he'd kill Sol and Sosa too. For losing. He told me he'd kill them both if I didn't fight, and if he finds out. . . ."

Var stood there having no answer.

"We weren't very smart, I guess," Soli said, beginning to cry.

He put his arm around her, feeling the same.

"I don't know enough about the nomads," she said. "I don't like being alone."

"Neither do I," Var said, realizing that it was exile he faced. Once he had been a loner and satisfied, but he had changed.

"Let's go together," Soli said.

Var thought about that, and it seemed good.

"Come on!" she cried, suddenly jubilant. "We can raid some other hostel for traveling gear and . . . and run right out of the country! Just you and me! And we can fight in the circle!"

"I don't want to fight you any more," he said.

"Silly! Not each other! *Other* people! And we can make a big tribe with all the ones we capture, and then come back and—"

"No! I won't fight the Master!"

"But if he's chasing you—"

"I'll keep running."

"But Var—!"

"No!" He shook her off.

Soli began to cry, as she always did when thwarted, and he was immediately sorry. But as usual he didn't know what to say.

"I guess it's like fighting your father," she said after a bit. That seemed to be the end of it.

"But we can still do everything else?" she asked wistfully after a bit more.

He smiled. "Everything!"

Reconciled, they began their flight.

By dusk they were ensconced in an unoccupied hostel twenty miles distant. "This is almost like home," Soli said. "Except that it's round. And everything's here. I guess the nomads haven't raided it this week."

Var shrugged. He was not at home in a hostel, but this had seemed better than foraging outside for supper. Alone, he would have stayed in deep forest; but with Soli. . . .

"I can fix us a real underworld meal," she said. "Uh, you *do* know how to use knives and forks? I saw how the cooks did it. Sosa says I should always be able to do for myself, 'cause sometime I might have to. Let's see, this is an electric range, and this button makes it hot."

One word stuck in his mind as he watched her busily

hauling out utensils and supplies. Sosa. That was the name of her stepmother, he knew. The little woman he had encountered underground, who had thrown him down so easily. The Master had spoken the name too. But there was something else—

Sos! Bob of the mountain had called the Master Sos! And so had Tyl, earlier; he remembered that now. As though the Nameless One *had* a name! And Sos would be the original husband of Sosa!

But Sol was married to Sosa, there in the mountain. And Sos was married to Sola. How had such a transposition come about?

And if Soli were the child of Sol and Sola, was there also a Sosi, born of Sos and Sosa? If so, where?

Var's head whirled with the complexity of such thinking. Somewhere in this confusion was the answer to the Master's strange wrath, he was sure. But how was he to untangle it?

Soli was having difficulties with their repast. "I need a can opener," she said, holding up a sealed can.

Var didn't know what a can opener was.

"To get these tomatoes open."

"How do you know what's in there?"

"It says on the label. T-O-M-A-T-O. The crazies label everything. That *is* what you call them, isn't it?"

"You mean you can read? The way the Master does?"

"Well, not very well," she admitted. "Jim the Librarian taught me. He says all the children of Helicon should learn to read, for the time when civilization comes back. How can I open this can?"

She called the mountain Helicon, too. So many little things were different! And she knew Jim the Gun's mountain brother, not the real Jim.

Var took the can and brought it to the weapons rack. He selected a dagger and plunged it into the flat end of the cylinder. Red juice squirted out, as though from a wound.

He took the dripping object back to her. It *was* tomatoes.

"You're smart," Soli said admiringly. It was ridiculous, but he felt proud.

Eventually she served up the meal. Var, accustomed in childhood to scavanging for edibles in ancient buildings and in the garbage dumps of human camps, was not particularly surprised at the food. He crunched on the burned meat and drank the tomatoes and gnawed on the fibrous rolls and sliced the rock-hard ice cream with the dagger. "Very good," he said, for the Master had always stressed the importance of courtesy.

"You don't have to be sarcastic!"

Var didn't understand the word, so he said nothing. Why was it that people so often got angry for no reason?

After the meal Var went outside to urinate, not used to the hostel's crockery sanitary facilities. Soli took a shower and pulled down a bunk from the wall.

"Don't turn on the television," she called as he reentered. "It's probably bugged."

Var hadn't intended to, but he wondered at her concern. "Bugged?"

"You know. The underworld has a tap so they know when someone's watching. Maybe the crazies do too. To keep track of the nomads. We don't want anyone to know where we are."

He remembered the Master's conversation with the mountain leader, Bob, and thought he understood. Television didn't *have* to be meaningless. He pulled down an adjacent bunk and flopped on it.

After a while he rolled over and looked at the television set. "Why is it so stupid?" he asked rhetorically.

"That's the way the Ancients were, before the Blast," she said. "They did stupid things, and they're all on tape, and we just run it through the transmitter and that's what's on television. Jim says it all means something, but we don't have the sound system so we can't tell for sure."

"We?"

"The underworld. Helicon. Jim says we have to maintain technology. We don't know how to *make* television, but we can maintain it. Until all the replacement parts wear out, anyway. The crazies know more about electricity than we do. They even have computers. But we do more work."

Var was becoming interested. "What *do* you do?"

"Manufacturing. We make the weapons and the pieces for the hostels. The crazies are Service; they put up the hostels and fill them with food and things. The nomads are consumers—they don't do anything."

This was too deep for Var, who had never heard of the underworld before this campaign and still had only the vaguest notion what the crazies were or did. "Why does the

Master have to conquer the mountain, if it does so much?"

"Bob says he's demented. Bob says he's a doublecrosser. He was supposed to end the empire, but he attacked the mountain instead. Bob's real mad."

"The Master said the mountain was bad. He said he couldn't make the empire great until he conquered the mountain. And now he says he'll burn it all, after he kills me."

"Maybe he *is* demented," she whispered.

Var wondered himself.

"I'm frightened," Soli said after a pause. "Bob says if the nomads make an empire there'll be another Blast and no one will escape. He says they're the violent element of our society, and they can't have technology or they'll make the Blast. Again. But now——"

Var couldn't follow that either. "Who made the mountain?" he asked her.

"Jim says he thinks it was made by post-Blast civilization," she said uncertainly. "There was radiation everywhere and they were dying, but they took their big machines and scooped a whole city into a pile and dug it out and put in electricity and saved their finest scientists and fixed it so no one else could get inside. But they needed food and things, so they had to trade—and some of the smart men outside had some civilization too, from somewhere, and they were the crazies, and so they traded. And everyone else, the stupid ones, just drifted and fought each other, and they were the nomads. And after a while too many men in Helicon got old and died, and technology was being lost, so they had to take in some others, but they had to keep it secret and the crazies wouldn't come, so they only took in the ones that came to die."

"I don't think the Master would make another Blast," Var said. But he remembered the man's mysterious fury, his threat to destroy all the mountain, and he wasn't sure.

Soli was discreet enough not to comment. After a time they slept.

Twenty miles away, the Nameless One, known by some as Sos, did not sleep. He paced his tent, sick with rage at the murder of his natural child, the girl called Soli, conceived in adultery but still flesh of his flesh. Since his time within the mountain he had been sterile, perhaps because of the operations the Helicon surgeon had performed on his body to make him the strongest man in the world. He carried metal under his skin and in his crotch, and hormones had made his body expand, but he could no longer sire a child. This Soli, legally the issue of the castrate Sol, was the only daughter he would ever beget, and though he had not seen her in six years she was more precious to him than ever. Any girl her age was precious, sympathetically. He had dreamed of reuniting with her and with his true friend Sol and with his own love Sosa, the four together, somehow—

But now such hopes were ashes. It was not a girl, but an entire foundation of ambition that had been abolished. Now the things of this world were without flavor.

Soli—perhaps she would have been like that gamin from Tribe Pan, alert and bold yet tearful, artfully so, when balked. But he would never know, for Var had killed her.

Var would surely die. And Helicon would be leveled, for Bob had engineered that ironic murder. No party to the event would survive, not even Sos the Weaponless, the most guilty of all concerned.

So he paced, ruled by his despairing fury, awaiting only the dawn to begin his mission of revenge. Tyl would supervise the siege of Helicon until his own return. Tyl at least would enjoy being in charge.

CHAPTER 13

In a month they were far beyond the Master's domains, but Var dared not rest. The Nameless One was slow but very determined, as Var had learned when they first met. He knew the local tribesmen would inform the Master of the route taken by the fugitive, so there was no escape except continued motion.

At first Soli had hidden whenever human beings were encountered, for she was officially dead. Then they realized that she could masquerade as a boy and even carry the sticks, and no one would know. So they traveled openly together, an ugly man and a fair boy, and no one challenged them.

They went west, for the Master's empire was east and Soli had heard that ocean lay to the south. Extensive desert badlands forced them north. They avoided trouble, but when it came at them relentlessly, they fought. Once a foul-mouthed sworder challenged Var, calling him a word he didn't know, but he got the gist and realized that it was supposed to be an insult. He met the sworder in the circle and flattened his nose and cracked his head with the sticks, and it was not pretty. Another time a small tribe sought to deny them access to a hostel; Var bloodied one, Soli a second, and the rest fled. The warriors beyond the empire were inept fighters.

In the second month they encountered so extensive a desert that they had to turn back. Fearing the Master, they took to the wilderness, avoiding the established trails.

But foraging while traveling these bleak hills was difficult. There was no time to set snares or to wait patiently for game. Soli had to turn girl child again to enter occupied

hostels for supplies, while Var skulked alone. She returned
with word that the Weaponless had passed this area two or
three days behind them. He was outside his empire now,
but no one could mistake the white-haired brute of a man.
He spoke only to describe Var and verify his transit and did
not enter the circle. He did not seem to be concerned about
Var's boy companion.

So it was true. The Master was on his trail, leaving everything else behind. Var felt fear and regret. He had hoped
that this murderous passion would fade, that the needs of
the mountain campaign would summon the Nameless One
back before very long. A minion might be dispatched to
finish the chore, of course; but Var would have no compunc-
tion about destroying such a man in the circle. It was only
the Master himself he could not bring himself to oppose, not
from fear, though he knew the Master would kill him, but
because this was, or had been, his only true friend.

Now he knew it was not to be. The Master would never
give up the pursuit.

They veered north, moving rapidly and sleeping in the
forest, the open plain, the tundra. Soli fetched supplies from
the hostels, sometimes as girl, sometimes as boy.

Yet the word spread ahead of them. When they encountered strangers accidentally they drew stares of semi-recog-
nition. "You with the mottled skin, aren't you the one the
juggernaut is after?" But such acquaintances usually did not
interfere, for Var was said to be devastating with the sticks.
And, in this region of haphazardly trained warriors, this was
a true description. The few who chose to challenge him in
the circle soon became limping testimony to this.

And few suspected that his boy companion was even better at such fighting, possessing both sophisticated stick technique and weaponless ability. Only when they had to fight
as a pair, against aggressive doubles, did this become evident.
Soli, adept at avoiding blows, fenced around and behind
Var, and the opposition was soon demolished.

In two more months of circuitous traveling they came to
the end of the crazy demesnes. The hostels stopped, and the
easy trails made by the crazy tractors terminated, and the
wilderness became total. And it was winter.

Undaunted, they plunged into the snowbound unknown. It
was an unkempt jungle of bare-boned trees, fraught with
gullies and stumbling stones hidden under the even blanket

of white. At dusk the snow began to fall again, gently at first, then solidly. Soli became grim and silent, for she was unused to this. Never before had she dealt with snow; she had never emerged from the mountain above the snowline. To her it had been something white but not necessarily cold or uncomfortable. Var knew the reality exasperated her and frightened her, catching at her feet and flying in her face.

Var excavated a pit, baring the unfrozen turf and making a circular wall of packed snow. He spread a ground sheet and pegged a low sturdy tent, letting the snow accumulate on top. He sealed it in except for a breathing tunnel and brought her inside, where he took off her boots, poured out the accumulated water and slapped at her feet until they began to warm. She no longer cried as freely as she had at their first meeting, and he rather wished she would, for now her misery just sat upon her and would not depart.

That night, after they had eaten, he held her closely and tried to comfort her, and gradually she relaxed and slept.

In the morning she would not awaken. Nervously he stripped her despite the cold, and dried her, and found the puncture mark: on the blue ankle just above the level of her unbooted foot. Something like a badlands moth had stung her, unobserved. They must have camped near a radiation fringe zone, far enough out so that his skin did not detect it, near enough for some of the typical fauna to appear. He might have recognized the area by sight had it not been snowing. Probably there were hybernating grubs, and one had been warmed into activity by her body and crawled and bit when disturbed. She was in a coma.

There was no herb he knew in this region in this season that would ease her condition. She was small; if she had taken in too much of the venom, she would sleep until she died. If she had a small dose, she would recover—if kept warm and dry.

The snowstorm had abated, but he knew it would return. At night it would be really cold again. This was no suitable place for illness, regardless. He had to get her to a heated hostel.

He struck tent, packed up everything hastily and carried her dangling over his shoulder, swathed in bag and canvas. He stumbled through the knee-deep snow, the hip-deep drifts, never pausing for a rest though his arms grew numb with the weight and his legs leaden.

After an hour he stepped into a snow-camouflaged burrow hole, stumbled, caught himself, caught Soli as she slid off his shoulder—and almost collapsed as the pain shot up his thigh. Then he went on as before, ignoring it, until the slower pain of his swelling ankle forced him to stop and remove his boot and rub snow on it. Then, barefooted, he continued.

After a time he had to stop again, to dispose of all superfluous weight. He hoisted Soli again and walked because he had to, no other reason. And before day was done he laid her limp body in the warm hostel, the last they had passed.

Soli's breathing was shallow, but she had neither the fever nor the chill of a serious illness. Var began to hope that he had acted in time and that the siege was light.

He rested beside her, the sensation in his leg coming through with appalling intensity. The wrench would not have been serious had he not continued to aggravate it, walking loaded. Now—

He heard something.

A man was coming up the walk to the hostel, treading the frozen path the crazies had cleared. Obviously intending to spend the night inside.

Var had had perhaps half an hour, hardly enough for strength to creep back into his limbs, more than enough to make his ankle a torment. But he dragged himself up, hastily winding a section of crazy sheet around his leg so that he could stand on it more firmly. He and Soli had remained hidden until this time, but he knew their secrecy would be gone if anyone saw her now. They had lost a day of travel, and the Master would be very close; any exposure could bring him here within hours.

The approaching steps were not those of the Weaponless. They were too light, too quick. But Var could tolerate no man inside this hostel, not while Soli lay ill, not while they both were vulnerable.

He scrambled into his heavy winter coat, pulled its hood tight around his face to conceal the discoloration above his beard, lifted his sticks, fought off the agony that threatened to collapse his leg and pushed through the spinning door to meet the stranger outside.

It was bright, though the day was waning; the snow amplified the angled sunlight and bounced it back and forth and across his squinting eyes. It took a moment to make out the intruder.

The man was of medium height, fair-skinned under the parka, and well proportioned. He wore a long, large knapsack that projected behind his head. His facial features were refined, almost feminine, and his motions were oddly smooth. He seemed harmless, a tourist wandering the country, broadening his mind, a loner. Var knew it was wrong to deny him lodging at the warm hostel, especially this late in the day, but with Soli's welfare at stake there was no choice. The Master could get the word and come before she recovered, and they would be doomed. He barred the way.

The man did not speak. He merely looked questioningly at Var.

"My—my sister is ill," Var said, aware that his words, as always with strangers, were hardly comprehensible. When he knew a person talking became easier, partly because he was relaxed and partly because the other picked up his verbal distortions and learned to compensate. "I must keep her isolated."

The traveler still was silent. He made a motion to pass Var.

Var blocked him again. "Sister—sick. Must . . . be . . . alone," he enunciated carefully.

Still mute, the man tried to pass again.

Var lifted one stick.

The stranger reached one hand over his shoulder and drew out a stick of his own.

So it was to be the circle.

Var did not want to fight this man at this time, for the other's position was reasonable. Var and Soli had fought together for their right to occupy any hostel at any time. Lacking an explanation, the other man had a right to be annoyed. And Var was in poor condition for the circle; only with difficulty did he conceal the liability of his leg, and he was quite tired generally from his day's labor. But he could not tell the whole truth and could not risk exposure. The man would have to lodge elsewhere.

It the stranger were typical of these outland warriors, Var would be able to defeat him despite his handicaps. Particularly stick against stick. Certainly he had to try.

The man preceded him down the path to the circle. This

was a relief, for it meant Var could conceal his limp while walking. The man kicked the circle free of loose snow, drew out his second stick, removed his tall backpack and his parka and took his stance. Suddenly he looked more capable; there was something highly professional about the way he handled himself.

Var, afraid to reveal his mottled skin, had to remain fully dressed, though it inhibited his mobility. He entered the circle.

They sparred, and immediately Var's worst fears were realized. He faced a master sticker. The man's motions were exceptionally smooth and efficient, his blows precise. Var had never seen such absolute control before. And speed—those hands were phenomenal, even in this cold.

Knowing that he had to win quickly if at all, Var laid on with fury. He was slightly larger than his opponent and probably stronger, and desperation gave him unusual skill despite his injury and fatigue. In fact, he was fighting better than ever before in his life, though he knew he would lose that edge in a few minutes as his resources gave out. At this moment, Tyl himself would have had to back off, reassess his strategy, and look to his defenses.

Yet the stranger met every pass with seeming ease, anticipating Var's strategy and neutralizing his force. Surely this was the finest sticker ever to enter the circle!

Then, abruptly, the man took the offense and penetrated Var's own guard as though it were nonexistent and laid him out with a blow against the head. Half conscious, Var fell backwards across the circle. He was finished.

His face sidewise in the snow, Var heard something. It was a noise, a shudder in the ground, as of ponderous feet coming down: crunch, crunch, crunch, crunch. An ear less attuned to the wilderness could not have picked it up, and Var himself would have missed it had his ear not been jammed to the land.

It was the distant tread of the Master.

The victor stood above him, looking down curiously.

"Stranger!" Var cried, half delirious. "Never have I met your like. I beg of you——" He was incoherent again, and had to slow down. "Let no man enter that hostel tonight! Guard her, give her time. . . ."

The man squatted to peer at him. Had he understood any

of it? It was unprecedented for the loser to beseech terms from the winner, but what else could he do now?

"A badlands grub—she will die if disturbed——" And Var himself would die if he didn't drag himself away immediately. Then who would take care of Soli? Would the Master linger to help her? Not while the vengeance trail was warm! No, it had to be this stranger, if only he would. Such exceeding skill in the circle had to be complemented by meticulous courtesy.

The man reached out to touch Var's injured leg. The sheet had come loose and a section of swollen skin showed. He nodded. This man would have won anyway, but he could not be pleased to discover he had fought a lame opponent. He stood and stepped out of the circle, leaving Var where he lay. He donned his parka, then his pack, putting the sticks away. He walked down the trail in the direction the Master was coming from.

He was leaving the cabin to Var.

Var did not question the stranger's act of generosity. He climbed to his feet and limped back to the cabin, turning several times to watch the man's departure. At last he entered and shut the door.

The stranger would meet the Master. Var was at his mercy now. Who was this silent one, and how had he come by such fabulous fighting skill? Var knew that no sticker in all the empire could match this warrior.

But the Master was not a sticker. What would pass between them when they met? Would they fight? Talk? Come to this cabin together? Or pass each other, and the Master would come to find the fugitives here?

Soli stirred, and he forgot all else. "Var . . . Var," she cried weakly, and he rushed to her side. She was recovering! It only they were granted the night—

They were. Though Var listened apprehensively for footsteps outside, no man came to the hostel.

In the morning Soli was well, though weak. "What happened?" she asked.

"You were stung by a badlands moth—its winter grub," Var said, though this was only conjecture. "It came alive when we warmed the ground, and got on you. I brought you here."

"What are those marks on you?"

"I fought a man who would intrude." And that was all he told her, lest she worry.

This time they picked up extra sheeting, so as to make possible a double layer on the ground and keep moisture and grubs out entirely. Var explained that they had lost time and had to move; he did not clarify how close he knew the Master to be, but she caught his urgency.

So they resumed their desperate trek. Soli was weak but she could walk. In her residual disorientation she was not aware of Var's limp.

As they left the hostel Var looked down the path once more, mystified. Who was the noble, dazzling, silent man who had made their escape possible? Would he ever know?

CHAPTER 14

They marched northward through winter and emerged at last in spring, far beyond the crazy domains. Here they found complete strangers: men and women who carried some guns and bows but not true weapons, and who did not fight in the circle, and who lived in structures resembling primitive, delapidated hostels. They burned wood to warm these "houses" because there was no electricity and illuminated them with smoky oil lanterns. They spoke an unpleasantly modulated dialect and were not especially friendly. It was as though every family were an island, cultivating its own fields, hunting its own preserve, neither attacking nor assisting strangers.

Still the Master followed, falling behind as much as a month, then catching up almost to within sight, forcing them to move out quickly. Now the silent man Var had fought accompanied the Nameless One. The scattered news reports and rumors described him well enough for Var to identify, though he said nothing to Soli about this. If she knew that a warrior of that quality had chosen to accompany the Master. . . .

Had those two fought, and the Master had made the stranger part of the empire? Or had they joined forces for convenience in the dangerous hinterlands?

Summer, and the country remained rugged and the pursuit continued. Soli was taller and stronger now, growing rapidly, and was quite capable. She learned from him how to make vine traps in the forest and capture small animals, and to skin them and gut them; how to strike fire and cook the meat. She learned to make a deadfall and to sleep com-

fortably in a tree. Her hair grew out black and fine, so that
she resembled her natural mother more than ever.

Soli taught him, in return, the rudiments of the weaponless combat she had learned from Sosa and the strategies
demonstrated by her father, Sol. For they both knew that
eventually the Master would catch up, and that Var, despite
his reservations, would have to fight. The Nameless One would
force the combat.

"But it's better to run as long as we can," she said, seeming to have changed her attitude over the months. "The
Weaponless defeated Sol in the circle long ago when I was
small, and Sol was the finest warrior of the age."

Var wondered whether Sol could have been so good as
the sticker now traveling with the Master, but he kept that
thought to himself.

"It was the Weaponless who struck my father on the
throat so hard he could not speak again," she said, as though
just remembering. "Yet you say they were friends."

"Sol does not speak?" Var's whole body tingled with an
appalling suspicion. He suddenly remembered the story she
had told him on the plateau, how her father had been
wounded and lost his speech.

"He can't. The underworld surgeon offered to operate, but
Sol wouldn't tolerate the knife. Not that way. It was as
though he felt he *had* to carry that wound. That's what
Sosa said, but she told me not to talk about it."

Var thought again of the fair stranger, the master sticker,
now almost certain that he knew the man's identity. "What
would your father do if he thought you were dead?"

"I don't know," she said. "I don't like to think about it,
so I don't. I miss him, and I'm really sorry—" But she
cut off that thought. "Bob probably wouldn't tell him. I
think Bob pretended I was being sent on an exploratory mission and didn't return. Bob almost never tells the truth."

"But if Sol found out—"

"I guess he would kill Bob, and—" Her mouth opened.
"Var, I never thought of that! He would break out of the underworld and—"

"I met him," Var said abruptly. "When you were ill. We
did not know each other. Now he travels with the Master."

"*Sol* is the Nameless One's companion? I should have realized! But that's wonderful, Var! They are together again.
They must really be friends."

Var told her the rest of the story: how he had fought
Sol and tried to send him back to oppose the Master. About
the strange generosity of the other man. "I did not know,"
he finished. "I kept him from you."

She kissed his cheek, a disconcertingly feminine gesture.
"You did not know. And you fought for me!"

"You can go back to him."

"More than anything else," she said, "I would like that.
But what of you, Var?"

"The Master has sworn to kill me. I must go on."

"If Sol travels with the Weaponless, he must agree with
him. They must both want to kill you now."

Var nodded miserably.

"I love my father more than anything else," she said slowly. "But I would not have him kill you, Var. You are my
friend. You gave me warmth on the mesa, you saved me
from illness and snow."

He had not realized that she attached such importance to
such things. "You helped me too," he said gruffly.

"Let me travel with you a while longer. Maybe I'll find a
way to talk to my father, and maybe then he can make
the Nameless One stop chasing you."

Var was immensely gratified by this decision of hers, but
he could not analyze his feeling. Perhaps it was this glimmer
of a promise of some mode of reconciliation with his mentor, the Master. Perhaps it was merely that he no longer felt
inclined to travel alone. But mostly it could be the loyalty
she showed for him, which filled an obscure but powerful
need that had made him miserable since the Master's turn-
about. To have a friend, that was the most important thing
there was.

The sea came north and fenced them in with its salty expanse. The pursuit closed in behind. The unfriendly natives
informed them with cynical satisfaction that they were
trapped: The ocean was west and south, the perpetual snows
north and two determined warriors east.

"Except," one surly storekeeper murmured smugly, "the
tunnel."

"Tunnel?" Var remembered the subway tunnel near the
mountain. He might hide in such a tube. "Radiation?"

"Who knows? No one ever leaves it."

"But where does it *go*?" Soli demanded.

"Across to China, maybe." And that was all he would tell them and probably all he knew.

"There's another Helicon in China," Soli said later. "That's not its name, but that's what it is. Sometimes we exchanged messages with them. By radio."

"But we are fighting the mountain!"

The Nameless One is fighting it. Or was. Sol isn't. We aren't. And this is a different one. It might help us, at least enough so I could talk to Sol. If we can find it. I don't know where it is in China."

Var remained uncertain but had no better alternative. If there was any way to escape the Master, he had to try it.

The entrance to the tunnel was huge, big enough to accommodate the largest crazy tractor or even several abreast. The ceiling was arched, the walls gently bowed, whether from design or incipient collapse Var was uncertain at first. But closer inspection revealed its complete sturdiness. There was solid dirt on the floor, but no metal rails. It was a dark hole.

"Just like the underworld," Soli said, undismayed. "There's an old subway beyond the back storage room with rats in it. I used to play there, but Sosa said there might be radiation."

"There was," Var said.

"How do you know?"

He summarized his foray to Helicon, before the first battle. "But the Master said she would tell them, so it would be booby-trapped. So we didn't use it."

"She never did. Bob knew it was there, but he said the geigers proved it was impassable, so he didn't worry about it. I guess the radiation was down when you came, but Sosa didn't say a word."

So they *could* have invaded that way! Why hadn't Sosa given the route away?

Then he remembered: Sos—Sosa. Sometime in the past she had been his wife, and she must still have loved him. So she hadn't told. But he had thought she had, and so the surface battle had begun. Just one more irony of many.

Soli lit one of their two lanterns and marched in. Var, perforce, followed.

Could this great tube actually cross under the entire ocean? What kept the water out, he wondered.

And why did no one emerge from it if other men had

entered? If the problem were radiation, he would discover it. But he feared that was not the case. There could be other dangers in fringe-radiation zones, as he knew so well. Mutant wildlife, from deadly moths to giant amphibians, as well as harmless forms like the mock-sparrow. And what else, here?

Deep in the tunnel the walls developed a tiled surface, clean and much more attractive than the bare metal and concrete. Var knew what had happened: The natives had pulled off the nearest tiles for their own use but had not dared to penetrate too far. The mud on the bottom also slacked off so that they walked on a fine gray surface of a coarse texture in detail but marvelously even as a whole. It was ideal for running; their feet had excellent traction.

But how far could this continue? After an hour's brisk walk, he asked Soli: "How wide is the ocean?"

"Jim showed me a map once. He said this way was the Pacific, and it's about ten thousand miles wide."

"Ten thousand miles! It will take years to cross!"

"No," she said. "You know better than that, Var. You can figure. If we walk four miles an hour, twelve hours a day, that's almost fifty miles."

"Twenty days to cover a thousand miles," he said, after a moment's difficult computation. "To cover ten thousand— over six months to cross it all. We have supplies for hardly a week!"

She laughed. "It isn't so wide up here. Maybe less than a hundred miles. I'm not sure. I think the tunnel must come up for air every so often, on the little islands. So we won't have to walk it all at one stretch."

Var hoped she was right. The tunnel was unnatural, and his nose picked up the dryness of it, the deadness. If danger fell upon them here, how could they escape?

They walked another hour, Soli swinging her lantern to make the grotesque shadows caper, and Var realized what it was that disturbed him most. The other tunnel, the subway passage, had teemed with life, though touched by radiation. This one had neither. Var knew that life intruded wherever it could and should be found in a protected place like this. What kept it clean? There had to be a reason, and not any swarm of shrews, for there were no droppings.

They rested briefly to eat and drink and leave the substance of their natural processes on the floor, since there was nowhere to bury it. They went on.

Then down the tunnel came a monster. It rumbled and hissed as it moved and shot water from its torso, and it was bathed in steam. A tremendous eye speared light ahead.

Var froze for a moment, terrified. Then his instincts took over. He backed and turned and started to run.

"No!" Soli cried, but he hardly paid attention.

As he plunged down the tunnel, she plunged too—and tackled him. Both fell, and the rushing glare played over them.

"Machine!" she cried. "Manmade. It won't hurt men!"

Now the thing was bearing down on them, faster than they could run, and the clank of its sparkling treads was deafening. It filled the passage.

"Stand up!" Soli screamed. "Show you're a man!" She meant it literally.

Var obeyed, unable to think for himself. Men seldom daunted him, but he had never experienced anything like this before.

Soli took his hand and stood by him, facing the machine. "Stop!" she cried at it, and waved her other hand in the blinding light, but it did not stop.

"Its recognition receptor must be broken!" she shouted, barely audible above the din, though her mouth was inches from his ear. "It doesn't know us!"

Var no longer had any doubts about what kept the passage clean. The water spouted out was probably a chemical spray such as the crazies used to clear pathways, which killed and dissolved anything organic. And men were organic.

They could not escape. The monster filled the tunnel, blasting its chemicals against the sides and ceiling, and he saw its front sweepers scooping dust into a hopper and wetting it down too. They could not get around it and could not outrun it. They had to fight.

Then it was upon them.

Var picked up Soli and heaved her into the air. As her weight left his arms, he leaped himself.

The machine struck.

Var clung to consciousness. He spread his arms and when one banged against something soft, he grasped it and fetched it in. He found a metal rod with the other hand and hung on to it.

He held Soli in his arms, and they were riding the machine, bodies spread against the warm headlight, feet braced against the upper rim of the hopper.

Once he was sure of his position, he checked Soli. She was limp. He hauled her about so that her head was against his; he put his ear to her mouth and felt the slight gout of air that proved she was breathing. He studied her head and body as well as he could, alternately blinded and shadowed by the cutting edge of light and found no blood. She was alive and whole, and if the concussion were not severe, she would awaken in time. All he had to do was hold her securely until the machine stopped.

He shifted about, hunkering down against the hopper rim. The brushes whirled in front, highlighted in the spillage of light, and the water poured down from nozzles, but still the air was foul with dust. Something not quite visible whirred and ground inside the yard-deep hopper, reminding him of gnashing teeth. He kept his feet out of it, certain that he perched precariously over an ugly death. He wrestled Soli around again and draped her over his thighs, supporting her shoulders with his free arm and her feet with one leg. He did not want any part of her to dangle into that dark maw.

His muscles grew tired, then knotted, but he did not shift position again. He knew it could not be long, at this speed, before the machine reached the end of the tunnel, and he knew by the packed dirt where it had to stop. It only cleaned so far, for some reason. Once it did stop, they could jump free. They would be the first to escape from this ferocious tunnel.

In less than half an hour light showed, a dim oval beyond the focus of the machine's beam. The vehicle ground to a halt, steam rising thickly about the wedged passengers. Var made his effort and discovered that his legs had gone to sleep.

Soli was still unconscious; there was no help there. If he dislodged himself now, he was likely to drop them both into the dread hopper.

The machine shuddered. The blasting water jets cut off. The grinder beneath Var ceased its motion, and he saw that his fear had been well founded. But at least now he could step down on those gears without losing his feet, and that would make it possible to recover his circulation and lever Soli out.

The light doused, leaving only the pale cast from the entrance. The machine jolted into motion again the other way. Soli rolled off, and Var had to grab for her. By the time he had her safe again, the motion was too swift. If he jumped with his prickling legs and her unconscious weight they would both be hurt.

But the grinder remained inert. Apparently it had been disconnected for the return trip, along with the spray and headlight. Var worked one foot down, then let Soli slide. Returning sensation made his legs painful, but now they were securely ensconced within the hopper, riding back along the tunnel at a good clip.

But why didn't she revive? Now, increasingly, he feared that she had struck her head too hard against the light and suffered brain damage. He had seen warriors who had become disorganized and even idiotic after club blows to the head. If that were the case with Soli. . . .

On and on the cleaner went, returning whence it had come. Var, helpless to do anything else, held Soli firm and slept.

He was jolted awake by bright light. The machine had come into the open. Soli still nestled unconscious in his arms.

The machine stopped again, and there were people. First men with strange weapons—no, they had to be tools—then tall, armed, armored women, peering in at him and Soli. Some carried round disks of stretched leather, so that one arm was fettered and useless for combat.

"Look at that!" one exclaimed wonderingly. "A beardface and a child."

Var did not speak immediately, sensing trouble. These women were aggressive, militant, unfeminine and unlike those he had seen before. Their curiosity did not seem friendly. Their metal helmets made them look like birds.

Soli did not move.

There was something guilty and ugly about their attitude, as though they were contemplating an intriguing perversion. Var drew out his sticks.

Immediately bows appeared and metal-tipped arrows were trained on him from several directions. He had no protection against these, and with Soli unconscious his position was hopeless. He dropped his weapons.

The quiet men were climbing on the machine, applying their tools to its surfaces. Evidently they cared for it the way the crazies cared for their tractors, checking it over after each trip. That was why it was still operating so long after its makers were gone.

"Out!" cried the burly woman who seemed to be the leader. She held a spear in one hand, a shield in the other.

Var obeyed, lifting Soli carefully.

"The child is sick!" someone cried. "Kill her!"

Var held Soli with one arm about her chest. With his other arm he grabbed for the leader of the females, catching her by her braided hair. He yanked her against him, hauling back on her head so that her neck was exposed. Her shield got in the way, making her struggles ineffective. He bared his teeth. He growled.

"Shoot him! Shoot him!" the captive woman screamed.

But the archers were oddly hesitant. "He must be a real man," one said. "The Queen would be angry."

"If my friend dies, I rip this throat!" Var said, breathing on the neck he held bent. He was not bluffing; his teeth had always been his natural weapon, even though they were clumsy compared to those of most animals.

Another woman came forward. "Let go our mistress; we will medicate the child."

Var shoved the captive away. She caught herself, rubbing her neck. "Take him to the Queen," she said.

A woman made as if to take Soli, but Var balked. "She stays with me. If you kill anyone, kill me first, because I will kill anyone who harms her." He had made an oath to that effect long ago, to Soli's natural mother, but that was not the reason he spoke as he did now. Soli was too important to him to lose.

They walked down a pathway toward water. Var saw that they were on a small island, hardly larger than required to serve as a surfacing point for the tunnel. The cleaning machine stood athwart the road, grinders and brushes and headlamps at each end, hissing and cooling as the mechanics labored over it. In this culture, it seemed, the men were crazies, the women nomad warriors. Well, it was their system.

Beyond the machine there was a level stretch; then the surface rose into a tremendous metal and stone bridge that traversed the extensive water and led out of sight.

At the waterside was a boat. Var and Soli had seen such floating craft in the course of their journey and understood their purpose, but they had never been really close to one. This boat was made of metal, and he did not understand why it did not sink, since he knew metal was heavier than water.

He balked at entering the craft but realized that there was no reasonable alternative. Obviously the Queen was not on this atoll. And if he made too much trouble, he and Soli both would die.

The boat rocked as they entered but held out the water. Var could see that its bottom deck was actually below the surface of the sea. One of the women pulled a cord, and a motor started banging and shaking. Then the entire thing nudged out from the dock.

It was astonishing that people other than the crazies or underworlders should possess and control motors. Yet obviously it was so.

The boat pushed along through the ocean. Var, unused to this rocking motion, soon felt queasy. But he refused to yield to it, knowing that any sign of weakness would further imperil himself and Soli.

How long would she sleep? He felt strangely unwhole without her.

The boat came to parallel the enormous bridge. Girders like those that rimmed the mountain Helicon projected from the sea and crossed and recrossed each other, forming an eye-dazzling network. But these were organized and functional, serving to support the elevated highway. Somewhere within this jumble that road was hidden; he could not see it now. He wondered why the amazons did not walk along it instead of splashing dangerously over the water.

At length they angled toward the bridge. There was an archway here, where the water under the span was clear for a space. And suspended in that cavity was something like a monstrous hornet's nest, all wood and rope and interleaved slices of metal and plastic and other substances Var could not guess at.

The boat drew up beneath this, where a blister hung scant feet from the surface of the water. A ladder of rope dropped down, and the women climbed up with alacrity to disappear within.

Var had to ascend carrying Soli. He laid her over his shoulder and grasped the ladder with one hand. It swung out, seeming too frail to bear the double load.

Well, if it broke he would swim. He was not really enthusiastic to enter the hive and did not trust these armored women. He hauled himself and his burden up, rung by rung, carefully curling his clumsy fingers about each. The rope did not break.

The ladder passed through a circular hole and was fastened above by a metal crosspiece. Var clung to this and got his feet to a board platform, and shifted Soli down. They were in a cramped chamber whose sides curved up and out. Metal cloth seemed to be the main element.

But there were other ladders to climb. Each level was larger, the curving walls more distant, until doors and intermediate chambers were all he could observe in passing.

At length they stood within a large room with adjacent compartments, rather like the Master's main tent.

On a throne fashioned of wickerwork sat the Queen: bloated, ugly, middle-aged, bejeweled. She wore a richly woven gown that sparkled iridescently. It fell from a high stiff collar behind her broad neck to the sides of her stout ankles and was open down the front.

Var, repulsed, averted his eyes.

Weapons threatened. "Foreign beardface, *look* at the Queen!"

He had to look; it seemed this was protocol. She reminded him of a figurine the Master had shown him once: a fertility goddess, artifact of the Ancients. The Master had said that in some cultures such a figure was considered to be the ultimate in beauty. But for Var the female attributes became negative when expanded to such grotesque proportions.

"Strip him," the Queen said.

Again Var had to make a decision. He could fight, but not effectively while supporting Soli, and both of them would be wounded or killed. Or he could submit to being stripped by these women. Nakedness was not a strong taboo with him, but he knew it was for others, and that the demand represented an insult. Still—

He yielded. "You promised to care for my friend," he said.

The Queen made an imperious gesture that sent gross quivers through her various anatomies. An unarmed woman came to take Soli. She brought her to a wicker divan and began checking the limp girl, while Var watched nervously. And the armed women removed his clothing.

"So he is whole," the Queen said, staring as though study-ing an animal.

The nurse attending Soli spoke: "Concussion. Doesn't look serious. Bruise on the neck, probably pinching a nerve, could let go anytime." She splashed water from a bowl on Soli's face.

The girl groaned. It was the first sound she had made since the leap to the tunnel sweeper, and Var felt suddenly weak with relief. If she could groan, she could recover.

"He looks strong," said the Queen. "But mottled. Do we want any piebalds?"

No one answered. Evidently the question was rhetorical.

After a moment she decided. "Yes, we'll try one." She pointed to Var. "Your Queen will honor you. Come here."

Prodded by spearlike arrows, Var walked toward her. He had some idea what she meant and was disgusted, but the weapons bristling about him discouraged overt protest. He saw Soli sitting up and wanted to go to her. If only he weren't restrained by the odds against him! Alone, he could have made a break, but he did not want to start trouble that would hurt the dazed girl.

He came to stand immediately before the gross Queen. She was even more repulsive up close. Fat jiggled on her body as she breathed, and there was a steamy unnatural smell about her.

She reached out and caught him with her grotesque hand. "Yes, your Queen will use you once, now—and no woman after her."

It was no longer possible to pretend to mistake her mean-ing. Var acted. He whirled on his guards, grabbing at their weapons, shoving the women down. He caught the handle of a fighting hatchet and raised the blade toward the Queen.

The guards fell back, for they could not mistake his mean-ing either. He could split her head before they reached him.

"Bring her!" Var cried, gesturing toward Soli. He hoped they would not realize that they could nullify his threat by threatening Soli.

Bows came up, arrows nocked. Var put both hands on the hatchet and poised above the Queen. Even if a dozen arrows transfixed him, he would take her with him.

Soli came, listless but walking by herself. She still wore her two sticks; they had not been noticed by her captors.

Something flashed. Var jumped back as the Queen drove at him with a jeweled stilletto.

In that moment of confusion, Var saw the arrows coming. One grazed his thigh. The guards closed in.

In a fury, Var leaped at the Queen and clove her head with a two-handed stroke. A cry of horror went up. He did not need to look. He knew as he yanked free the blood-soiled blade that she was dead.

He caught Soli by the arm and sprinted for the nearest compartment behind the throne. For a moment no one followed. The women were too shocked by the fate of their breeder Queen.

There was a ladder. "Climb!" he cried at Soli, and she, unspeaking, climbed. Var stood with the hatchet, ready to fend off attack. He was sure that he himself would never have the chance to use the ladder.

Then, as the amazons advanced keening in fury, he struck at the wicker door supports. Rope and fiber sliced easily, the door began to collapse and the floor beneath it sagged. He hacked some more until there was a tumble of material sealing him off, then dived for the ladder.

Soli waited for him at the next level. "Where are we, Var?" she asked plaintively.

"In a hive!" he gasped, drawing her through another door. "I killed the Queen ant!"

They entered another large room. Men were working here, weaving baskets. Naked, flabby—Var saw at once that they were castrate. No wonder the women had been fascinated by the visiting male—they seldom saw a complete man!

But though these men were harmless, even pitiful, the amazon women were not. They burst through the door behind screaming.

Var and Soli bolted again. But the next room was a blank cubbyhole, next to the gentle curvature of the exterior wall. They were trapped.

"Fire!" Soli cried.

Var cursed himself for not thinking of that sooner. He fumbled for his pack for a precious match and some kerosene. This dry hive would ignite rapidly.

His pack, of course, was not on him. It lay with the rest of his clothing in the Queen's hall.

But Soli was already making fire from the duplicate materials in her own pack. As the first female warrior charged into the compartment, she ignited a puddle of kerosene on the wooden floor.

The amazon stomped through the sudden blaze and screamed. Var clove her with the hatchet and she fell, her shield rolling away, the fire licking around her body.

"We're trapped, Var!" Soli cried. For the moment he was too glad to have her intelligible and functional to pay attention to her words. Perhaps the action had jolted her out of her concussion.

"We'll burn!" she screamed in his ear.

That registered. He went to the wall and began hacking. The fibers were tough, and several times the blade rang against metal, but he succeeded in ripping a hole to daylight.

"Hurry!" Soli cried, and he glanced at her while chipping. He saw to his surprise that the fire was not consuming everything. Only the kerosene itself was burning. Soli stood just behind it, both sticks in her hands, fending off any Amazons who tried to reach through. Fortunately the constriction of the surroundings prevented the effective use of arrows. But soon the flammable fluid would be gone, and the mass of outraged women would press through. Some were already trying to use their shields to block Soli's sticks.

"Out the hole!" Var shouted at her. Soli obeyed with alacrity while he covered her retreat.

He took a final swipe at a protruding spear and dived through the hole the moment her feet disappeared. As his head poked out he saw the water far below. He had forgotten how high they were! How could they jump that dizzying distance?

Where was Soli? He did not spy her either on the wall or in the water. If she had fallen and drowned—

"Here!"

He looked up. She was clinging to the framework above the hole. Again, relief was almost painfully great.

And of course climbing was the answer. They could escape via the rope that supported the entire framework!

A helmeted head showed in the hole. Soli reached down negligently and tapped it ringingly with a stick. It vanished.

They climbed, Var carrying the hatchet between his teeth. It was easier than the ascent to the mesa had been, so long ago in experience. The woven ropes and struts provided plentiful handholds, and as the two rose the surface tilted toward the horizontal.

A trapdoor opened in the top and a head appeared. Var threatened it with the hatchet and the lid popped closed again instantly. They had command of the roof.

The rope by which the hive was suspended was much more sturdy than it had appeared from a distance. It was a good four feet in diameter at its narrowest, and the fibers were metal and nylon and rubber, interwoven tightly.

Var had had some notion of chopping through this cord and dropping the entire hive grandly into the sea. He gave it up; his battered little hatchet could not do the job.

They climbed the column, Soli still wearing her heavy pack because there was no time for adjustments. Fortunately this stretch was short. Var didn't know how long she could last, after her prolonged unconsciousness. And if the amazons emerged and started firing arrows at them—

The women did emerge, but too late. Var and Soli were perched on the massive steel strut that supported the hive, and the arrows could not reach them directly. They were safe. All they had to do was mount the road surface of the bridge and be on their way.

Well, not *quite* all. A chill wind attacked Var's bare skin. He would have to find new clothing and traveling supplies. And new weapons. This hatchet, useful as it had been, was not to his liking.

He led the way up an inclined beam, going into the maze of supports. The angry cries of the amazons were left behind, and their arrows stopped rattling between the girders. He wondered why they did not follow; certainly they would know how to get around on the bridge since they had built their hive within it.

His skin burned. First he thought it was windchap. Then he recognized the stigma of radiation.

"Back!" he cried, knowing Soli could not feel it, but would surely be affected. "Radiation!"

They retreated to a clean spot, where intersecting beams formed a gaunt basket. Now they knew why the amazons had not pursued them here. The women must have learned the hard way that the bridge was impassable. In fact, they must have constructed their vulnerable hive in the one place they knew to be safe from all marauders.

Var knew what he would find: the bridge ahead would be saturated with the deadly rays, making it a badlands. Probably some radiation touched in between the hive and the island where the tunnel emerged too—but even if not, the amazons would be waiting at the island with drawn bows.

Soli, so brave until this point, suddenly gave out. She laid her head against Var's shoulder and cried. She had not done that for many months.

The wind was colder now, and night was coming.

CHAPTER 15

It was an uncomfortable night. Soli's pack contained food and some clothing, so Var was able to fortify himself somewhat internally and externally. But the hardness and narrowness of the beams, the cutting edge of the intermittent wind, their several flesh wounds and the general hopelessness of their situation made sleep a misery.

They clung together as they had done on the mesa of Muse, and they talked. "Does your head hurt?" Var asked, trying to make the inquiry seem more casual than it was.

"Yes. I think I banged it. How did we get out of the tunnel?"

Var told her.

"I think I started to wake when you made me stand," she said. "I heard voices, and something shook me, but it was all very far away, maybe a dream. Then I woke again and saw water, but I didn't know what was happening so I didn't move. I was pretty much alert when you carried me into the hive, but then I *knew* I had to stay out of trouble. I kept my eyes closed, so I didn't really know what it was."

That explained how she had been able to function almost normally once she woke up officially. She had been smart enough to play dead until she knew more. It had been hard on Var, but he knew that it would have been worse any other way. The amazons had treated him more carefully because they knew he was not much of a threat while he held the unconscious girl.

"Those men," she said. "They were almost like my father, Sol, except that he's no weakling."

Var was aware of that. "They're castrates."

"But those hive-men—how could they—?" she asked.

115

He didn't know and did not want to conjecture. It was an awkward subject to discuss with any female, particularly a nine, almost ten-year-old child.

"What are we going to do, Var?" she asked after a while.

"When it gets light we can climb down to the water and swim. Maybe we can get around the radiation."

"I don't know how to swim."

She had been brought up in the mountain. She would never have had the chance to sport in open water, he realized. And in the summer and winter and summer they had traveled together, they had never had occasion to swim. What were they to do now?

"Will you teach me, Var?" she asked shyly.

Again she had provided the answer herself. "I will teach you," he agreed.

Finally they did sleep. The wind died down and that was better.

The amazons, as though confident of their quarry, were not on watch in the morning. Var and Soli descended to the water with some difficulty, as the girders merged into isolated smooth pylons and plunged into the sea. He showed her the motions of swimming in the cold water and told her to keep her head up. She mastered the art quickly, though she splashed a good deal and stayed very close to him. "It's so deep!" she explained. They set out west along the bridge.

The radiation came, and they veered out into the ocean. This frightened Soli, but they both knew there was no other way. After a time he treaded water while she clung to him, exhausted. He could not tell whether the droplets on her face were from the sea or her eyes. Certainly she was tired, tense and miserable.

Var wondered whether it would be feasible to steal a boat, but decided negatively. They wanted to hide, not advertise their presence by such activity. They would be safest on the bridge once they got past the radiation.

Progress was slow. Several times they came all the way in to a pylon safely and hung on while Soli coughed out mouthfuls of salt water. Her lips were blue and her face forlorn. Finally Var mounted a pylon and climbed stiffly until he encountered the radiation. They had to continue swimming.

But on the second try, half an hour later, he found no radiation. He helped her up. The sun came out and they soaked up its warmth as they ate sodden bread from the pack.

Then on down the highway, marching along its level thread toward China. Their supplies had been halved by the loss of Var's pack, but he thought they might catch some fish. And if there were other islands, there might be fruit or berries or at least rats.

Later in the day the road descended to land, and it was a larger island, many miles across, with trees and seals and birds and houses.

But they were wary, for there could also be men here, and the hive experience had taught them not to trust their own kind. Var had not before appreciated the true strength of the crazy-nomad system and still did not comprehend its mechanisms. But somehow men were civilized there, as they were not at the hive. A man did not have to worry about castration or fight outside the circle in America.

There were no people. The island was vacant. They found old cans of food but did not touch these. A few berries grew in patches, and these provided a supplement to their pack supplies. One of the houses seemed reasonably tight, and so they set up there after driving out the rats. (Soli said she'd rather not eat any rats just yet.)

At dawn the sound of a motor approached. They hid, watching through a dirt-crusted window that still had glass, and saw a boat with amazons pull up to the shore. This island was their foraging ground.

The women stepped out and surveyed the area efficiently. Evidently they did not come here often, or they would not have needed to check it out so carefully. Fortunately they did not approach the house where Var and Soli lurked. Then several of the castrated men emerged. They were herded to one of the berry areas and put to work picking berries and dropping them into wicker baskets, while the armored women took turns practicing with their weaponry.

After a couple of hours the baskets were full and the men returned to the boat. Var and Soli relaxed. Then they tensed again, for two people came ashore and headed for the houses. A young man and a woman. They walked slowly, the man leading and listless, the woman prodding him along every so often.

"This one," she said, stopping at a house. She jerked open the door. Wood and plaster crashed down, and she coughed in the dust.

She tried the next house, but the door was jammed. She

was a hefty woman, quite stout under her armor, but the house was sealed. Var had had the same experience the night before.

Then the amazon came to the one Var and Soli occupied.

The fugitives scrambled for the back room as the door pushed open. Var scooped up the pack, Soli their scattered belongings.

"Good," the amazon said as the door opened. "This one's tight and even fairly clean. You'd hardly know it's been deserted for years."

Var controlled his breathing and peered out of the gloom of the back room. Soli did the same. There was a back exit —they had made sure of that before settling in—but that door creaked, and if they used it now they would be discovered. Then they would have to kill the two visitors, and the hunt would be on again, with no radiation to hide behind. And other couples were entering neighboring houses; he could hear them. Any noise would bring them running. Better to wait it out.

"Strip," the woman said, as imperiously as her erstwhile Queen. The man obeyed with resignation. Var saw that the man had been mutilated, but not castrated.

Now the woman stripped, helmet to greaves. She stood and smiled.

And Var realized: they had come here to make sex! And the other couples would be doing the same. He looked across at Soli, wondering what her thoughts were. Her face was concealed in the shadow.

"There will have to be a new Queen," the amazon murmured, leading the man to the worn mattress Var had slept on. "I have borne four healthy girls. One more and I will be in contention as a breed-leader and can claim the Queenship —after I kill the other claimants. You, my pretty, have given me two of those girls, and you shall be well rewarded if you give me another."

"Yes," said the man unenthusiastically.

"Of course, if you disappoint me with a boy, it will go hard with you."

The man nodded.

Var, to his dismay, felt a surge of curiosity. He would have liked to see what transpired. It was awful—but compelling.

Var, too intent on listening, lost his balance and fell into the room.

Then it was rapid. Committed, Var and Soli had to strike. Almost before Var realized what had happened, the amazon pair lay sprawled unconscious, and there were shouts from the boat and other cabins in response to the noise of the brief battle. Var took up the amazon's bow and arrows and Soli her spear; they grabbed their own possessions as well and ran out the back.

Despite the strait his guilty curiosity had brought them to, Var regretted that he had not learned how the amazons mated. Would he ever know?

Armed women were charging from the boat and emerging, rumpled, from houses. Five of them were headed toward Var and Soli, while the men milled uncertainly on the shore. Three were closing in on the house just vacated. Two split off to cover the path to the bridge. Var saw that that route was hopeless. In fact, now that the hornets had been aroused, the entire island was hopeless. The women were tough, and odds of five to two in daylight were prohibitive. And the men would naturally assist their females.

"The boat!" Soli whispered piercingly. "This way!"

Var knew that direction to be the very height of folly. But she was already running at right angles to the path of the approaching trio, and he had either to follow or to let her go alone. He could not call to her, for that would pinpoint their location immediately. So he followed.

She circled toward the boat. The amazons, not suspecting this maneuver, remained in the village. He could hear them exclaiming over the fallen couple and banging through the houses in that section. Soli stopped just before they came in sight of the men.

"They're weaklings," she gasped. "The men don't fight. If we run at them and yell, they'll flee." And she set off again, running and yelling and waving her arms.

Var had to follow once more.

The men did scatter, though there were four of them here, all full grown. Var marveled.

"Now the boat!" Soli said, clambering in.

As Var settled beside her, the amazons realized what had happened and gave hue and cry.

"Start the motor!" Soli yelled at him.

He looked at her blankly.

"The pull cord!" she cried. She grabbed a handle on the engine and jerked. It came out on a string, and there was a bang. Var remembered that he had seen an amazon do this on the other boat that took them to the hive.

He took hold and gave it a tremendous yank. The cord came out a yard and the motor roared.

"I'll steer!" Soli screamed over the noise. She grabbed a wheel in the middle of the boat and began doing things with handles there. To Var's amazement, the craft began to move. She knew what she was doing!

Under Soli's guidance, it nudged out from the bank and swashed into deeper water. The amazons ran up, brandishing their spears, but there was twenty feet of water separating them from the boat. Then the women kneeled and lifted their bows.

Soli jerked another handle and the motor multiplied its sound. The boat jumped forward.

The arrows came. They were not random shots. They passed well wide of the engine section, which the archers did not want to damage, and centered on the personnel. They did not miss by much. Only Soli's sudden burst of speed spoiled their aim.

The second volley was already nocked, and Var knew this one would score, though the boat was not fifty feet away and moving swiftly. He grabbed one of the round amazon leather shields and held it behind Soli's back, for she could not see the arrows coming while she was driving.

Three arrows plonked into the shield, surely fatal to her had they not been intercepted. Two struck Var. One was in his right arm, rending flesh and bone; the other was in his gut.

He clung to consciousness, for they were not out of danger yet. He left the arrows where they were, but shifted the shield to his left hand and kneeled behind Soli, protecting her by both his shield and his body.

Two more arrows plunged into the leather, their points coming through but without much force. Another skewered his unprotected thigh. One more passed just beside his head and struck the wood near Soli.

"Var, can't you——" she said, turning.

Then she saw his situation and screamed.

Var passed out.

CHAPTER 16

He woke and fainted many times, conscious of pain and
the passage of time and the rocking of waves and Soli's
attentions, and of very little else. The arrows were out from
his arm and leg and gut, but this brought him no relief. His
body was burning, his throat dry, his bowels pressing.

She took care of him. She propped him up inside the boat's
cabin and held water to his mouth, and it made him sick and
the heaves wrenched his abdomen cruelly, but his lips and
tongue and throat felt better. He soiled himself many times
and she cleaned him up, and when she washed his genitals
they reacted and that made him ashamed but there was
nothing he could do. He kept bleeding from his wounds, and
she would wash them and bandage them, and then he would
move and the blood would flow hotly again.

He thought deliriously of the Master in the badlands seven
years before, his illness from radiation. Now Var knew what
the man had gone through and why he had sworn friendship
to the wild boy who had aided him then. But the thought
brought another torment, for he still could not fathom why
the Master had reversed that oath and become a mortal
enemy.

But most of all, he thought of Soli, she who cared for him
now in his helplessness. A child yet, but a master sticker
and faithful companion who had never remarked on the colors
of his skin or the crudity of his hands and feet and hunch. She
could have returned to her father, whom she loved, but had
not. She could even have gone to the Master, who had offered
to adopt her as his daughter. Such offers were never casually
made. She had stayed with Var because she thought he
needed help.

And he did.

It was night, and he slept. It was day, and he moved fitfully and half slept, hearing the roaring of the motor, smelling the gasoline she poured from stacked cans into the funnel. It was night again and cold, and Soli hugged him close and wrapped rough blankets about them both and warmed him with her small body while his teeth knocked together.

But he did not recover.

In one of his lucid moments—and he was aware they were not frequent—she talked with him about the mountain Helicon and the nomads.

"You know, I thought you people were savages," she said. "Then I met you and the Nameless One, and I knew you were merely ignorant. I thought it would be good to have you joined with underworld technology."

"Yes . . ." He wanted to agree, to converse on her level, sure he was able to do so now. But the sentence played itself out in silence.

"But now I've seen what it's like beyond the crazy demesnes, where the common man does have some technology, and I'm not so sure. I wonder whether the nomads would lose their primitive values, if—"

Yes, yes! He had wondered the same. And been unable to express it succinctly. The amazons and their motors and their barbarism. . . . But he could remember no more of that fragment. The boat went on and on beside the bridge. Once he felt radiation and cried out, and she veered away from it.

Then time had passed or stopped and the boat was docked and there were people. Not amazons, not nomads. Soli was gone and then she was back, crying, and she kissed him and was gone again.

A man came and stabbed him in the arm with a spike. When Var woke once more, his abdomen hurt with a different kind of hurt, a mending hurt, and he knew he was at last recovering. But Soli was not there.

Women came and fed him and cleaned him, and he slept some more. And days passed.

"I believe you are well now," a stranger said one day. He was old enough to be losing his hair and somewhat stout and flabby. No warrior of the circle, he!

Var *was* well, though weak. His arm and leg and gut had

healed, and he was now able to eat without vomiting and to eliminate without bleeding. But he did not trust this man, and he missed Soli, who had not come again since the time she kissed him and cried.

"The girl, what is your relationship to her?" the man asked.

"We are friends."

"You speak with a heavy accent. And you appear to have suffered serious radiation burns at one time and childhood deformities. Where do you come from?"

"Crazy demesnes," he answered, remembering Soli's term.

The man frowned. "Are you being clever?"

"Some call it America. The crazies share it with the nomads."

"Oh." The man brought him strange, elegant clothing. "Well, you should be advised that this is New Crete, in the Aleutians. We are civilized, but we have our own conventions. The girl understands this but feels that you may not."

"Soli—where is she?"

"She is at the temple, awaiting the pleasure of our God. You may see her now if you wish."

"Yes." Var still did not like the man's attitude. It was not exactly cynicism of the Helicon vintage, but it wasn't friendly either.

He dressed, feeling awkward in the long loose trousers and long-sleeved white shirt and particularly in the stiff leather shoes that hurt his clubbed feet. This was not what Var considered to be civilized attire. But the man insisted that he wear these things before going out.

They were in a city, not a dead badlands city, but a living metropolis with lighted buildings and moving vehicles. People thronged the clean streets. Var felt less uncomfortable when he saw that most men were garbed as he was.

The temple was a tremendous building buttressed by columns and a high wall. Guards armed with guns stood at the front gate. Var, so weak that even the short walk fatigued him, and weaponless, felt nervous.

Within the temple were robed priests and elaborate furnishings. After several challenges and explanations, Var's guide brought him to a chamber whose center was crossed by a row of vertical metal bars, each set about four inches from its neighbor.

Soli entered the other half of the room. She saw Var and

ran up to the bars, reaching through to grasp his hand. "You're all right!" she cried, her voice breaking.

"Yes." He was not so certain about her. She looked well, but there was something wrong about her manner. "Why are you here, behind these bars?"

"I'm in the temple." She was silent a moment, just looking at him. "I agreed to do something, so I have to stay here. I can't see you again after this, Var."

He was not facile with words. He did not know how to protest eloquently, to make her tell the truth. Particularly not with the stranger listening. But he knew from her tight, controlled, desperate manner that something terrible had happened while he lay sick, and that Soli expected never to see him again.

And she did not want him to know why.

She had been alienated from him as surely as had the Master—and also by the agency of some third party.

"Good-bye, Var."

He refused to say it to her. He squeezed her hand and turned to go, knowing that this was not the occasion for effective rebuttal. He knew too little.

And during the walk back he worked out what he had to do.

"You will have to go to the employment agency and make application for training," the man said. "Even the menial jobs will be complicated for you at first."

"What if I want to leave here?" *Not without Soli, though!*

"Why of course you may, if you purchase a boat and supplies. This is a free island. But to do that you will need money."

"Money?"

"If you don't know what that is, you don't have any."

Var let that pass. In time he would find out what money was and whether he needed it. It sounded like some variation of barter, however.

They entered the hospital and returned to Var's room. "You'll be moving out of here in a day or so," the man said.

Var looked around. None of his or Soli's possessions were in evidence, except the bracelet he wore, and that was dull and scratched. He thought he knew why they hadn't taken that: They didn't know it was gold.

The bed was similar to some he had seen during his childhood in the badlands. It had high rods of metal projecting at either end, rather like the grates to certain Ancient windows or the bars in that temple room. Generally, these could be screwed loose. . . .

"And a final word," the man said. "Don't go bothering them at the temple. They won't let you see your friend again."

Var placed a hand on one of the rods and twisted. It was tight. "Why not?"

"Because she is now a temple maiden, dedicated to our god, Minos. These girls are kept in seclusion for the duration."

Var tried another bar. This one turned. "Why?"

"Regulations. When they approach nubility, there is too much danger of their losing their value to the god."

The rod came free. Var held it aloft and advanced on the man, suppressing a tremor of weakness. *"What will happen to her?"*

The man looked at him and at the improvised club as though ignorant of the threat. "Really, there is no need for that—"

"Tell me or you die." Var, driven by fear for Soli, was not bluffing. He was weak, but this man was obviously untrained for combat. One or two blows would suffice.

"Very well. She is to be sacrificed to Minos."

Var wavered, suddenly feeling his weakness redoubled. His worst fear had been brutally confirmed. "Why?"

"You were dying. Medical attention is expensive. She agreed to enter the temple—it has to be voluntary, for we are civilized—if we made you well again. Because she will be lovely, and the god likes that, we acceded to the unusual commitment. Today we demonstrated that we kept our bargain, and now she will keep hers."

"She will—die?"

"Yes."

Var dropped the bedpost and sat down, befuddled and horrified. "How—"

"She will be chained to the rock at the entrance to the labyrinth. Minos will come and devour her in his fashion. Then fortune will smile on New Crete for one more month, for our god will be satisfied."

One last thing Var had to know. "When—"

"Oh, not for a couple of years yet. Your friend is still a

child." He glanced obscurely at Var. "Otherwise I dare say she would not have proved eligible."

Var did not follow the man's nuances and did not care to. The relief was as debilitating as the threat. Two years! There were a thousand things he could do to save her in that time.

"Remember, nomad, she made a bargain. Young as she is, she strikes us as a person of integrity. She will not break her vow that saved your life, no matter what you may do."

And that, Var realized with dismay, was the truth. Soli had always been keen to keep a bargain, any bargain. She didn't object to little ploys, such as passing for a boy or stealing the food they needed to live on, but she liked the formal things to be right.

The man stood up. "I know it is hard for you to accept the ways of an unfamiliar culture, just as I would have trouble adapting to your crazy-circle system of America." Var noted that the man, despite his earlier attitude, did after all know something of nomad existence. Maybe Soli had told him, and he had been verifying it with Var. "But you will find us fair and even generous if you cooperate with the system. Tomorrow you will be released, and I'll direct you to the employment agency. They will test you for aptitude and provide the indicated training. From then on, it is up to you. If you work well, you will eat well."

He left.

Var lay on the bed. He appreciated the efficiency of the system—it had points of similarity to the empire—but he had no intention of letting Soli die.

Still, he did have time to plan carefully. Until he came upon a suitable course of action, he could afford to cooperate.

Var became a trash collector. Because he was ugly and the proffered training perfunctory, he could not aspire to any prestige position. Because he was illiterate and had poor hands, he could not handle most of the more sophisticated jobs of New Crete, a literate, technological soceity. And hauling refuse on a daily basis kept him in excellent physical condition. People left him alone because of the dirt and the smell, and that was the way he wanted it too. He had a room with running water and heat in the winter and even an electric light that snapped on when he yanked at a string, and he earned enough of the metal tokens that were "money" to purchase clothing and regular meals and occasional entertainment.

It was a year before he discovered just how valuable his golden bracelet of manhood was here. He had thought it would bring a few of their silver tokens, but the truth was that had it been appraised and sold it would have paid for all his initial hospitalization. Gold, so common in the crazy demesnes, was at a premium here, for they used it in their machinery in ways he did not understand. Soli must have suspected this yet sold herself into the temple rather than take advantage of it.

Her generosity had been foolish. A man wore the bracelet only to give it to the woman of his choice. What could she care whether he wore it? He had no woman to give it to.

By day Var cooperated and had no trouble. By night he stripped his conventional clothing, dressed in warm rags, and ranged barefoot in the wilderness regions of New Crete. The island was large, at least twenty miles across, and he was able to explore it without disturbing the inhabitants, and to practice his weaponry. He made himself a fine set of sticks from seasoned wood and became as proficient with them as he had ever been in the circle with the metal ones. It was not the implement but the skill of the hand that counted. He learned the lay of the land and even ventured some distance into the dark tunnel that left the island on the west. It was clogged with refuse; no mechanical sweepers cleaned it, and it had been used as a dump.

And he scouted the temple preserve. This was a walled enclosure between one and two miles in diameter, patrolled but not heavily. Var had no problem sneaking in. Every day the maidens were exercised, Soli among them, and Var observed that she was well cared for. Every month at full moon one of the older ones was taken to a canyon and chained there. Next evening she would be gone. Var never actually saw the god Minos, because the god struck not by the light of that full moon, oddly, but by day. The maidens were put out before dawn and remained as it grew light. Var could not do so; he had to work by day, every day, and had he remained in the compound he would have run the double risk of absence at his assigned location and discovery at his forbidden location.

In the second year he built a boat. Not a good one, not nearly as good as the amazon one they had arrived in (what had happened to it? Why hadn't *that* value been charged against his medical bill?) and certainly not one he would trust to the open seas. Even if he were sailor enough to manage it. But the craft would do to spirit Soli away and hide her until better arrangements could be made. First he had to save her from Minos.

For if she were chained in the canyon for the god, then rescued, her bargain would be complete. She would have offered herself in sacrifice and found unexpected reprieve. All he had to do was stop Minos from eating her, then take her away, and the temple would never know the difference.

The morning came. Var was watching, for he knew the monthly date of the ceremony (he could look at the moon as well as a priest could) and had been aware that her turn was incipient. Most of the girls were now younger than she, and the temple did not provide board and keep longer than necessary. This was the day he would not go on his rounds—indeed, not ever again.

Soli, grown barely nubile in two years, was taken by hooded priests to the canyon and anchored there. The men—Var could not be certain of their sex, but assumed this was man's business—hammered spiked shackles into the stone. Soli's slender wrists were pinned within them at shoulder height. He had not seen Soli for so long, and now she had come to look remarkably like her natural mother Sola.

He lurked in the trees as the priests departed. He waited half an hour, making sure they would not return and that no other parties were watching. The canyon face was shielded from the direct view of the temple, probably intentionally and mercifully for the remaining maidens. Var now knew how most of them came here: They volunteered in order to spare their families hunger, for there were many poor people on the island. The he-who-won't-work-won't-eat philosophy was a thin cover for subjugation of the unfortunate. The wage that had been adequate for Var was not enough for a family, so there was continual and large-scale distress. The way of the crazies and the nomads was better, for no one hungered in America.

Assured that he was unobserved, Var let fly his random philosophies, emerged from hiding and entered the canyon. Soli heard him and looked up with a poignant little cry of dismay, thinking the god had come already. Then she gasped. "Var!"

He approached and put his hand to one manacle. "I never forgot you," he said. "Did you think I would let you be eaten?"

But the bond was tight, and he had no leverage to pry it loose.

"I—" she started, her eyes suddenly streaming. "I—thank you, Var. But I can't go with you. I made a vow."

"You fulfilled it!" He cast about for some way to get the metal out of the stone. Why hadn't he anticipated this detail?

"No. Not until the sacrifice," she said.

Var yanked at the other manacle. There seemed to be some give in it.

"I can't let you do this," she said through her tears.

Var ignored her and continued to work on the metal. His sticks would not pry it, being too thick to squeeze in beside her wrist, and the outside offered no help. He might hammer the metal with a stone, but the sound would bring the priests, or Minos himself.

Then he was thrown back.

Soli had raised her bare foot and shoved him hard in the chest. Now he understood: She meant it. She would resist him physically, not permitting him to labor on the bonds.

That meant he could not free her unless he knocked her out. And what kind of cooperation would she give him thereafter if he violated her oath by such force?

In any event, he could not bring himself to strike her. Anyone else, yes; Soli, no.

He stood up and faced her. "Then I'll go slay Minos," he said.

"No!" she screamed in horror. "He's a beast! No one can hurt him!"

"I have sworn to kill the man who harms Sola's child," Var said. "I swore it long before you made *your* oath. Would you have me wait until after the—after the creature comes?"

"But Minos is a god, not a man! You can't kill him!"

"He devours maidens—but he's not a beast?" Then he was ashamed of his irony with her. "Whatever he is, I must meet him unless you come with me now."

"I can't."

Var saw that further argument was useless. He marched down the canyon into the labyrinth, heedless of her low cries.

There was a large, open cave where the walls merged. From its rear several smaller passages opened. Var held his sticks up and went cautiously into one.

It led to a medium chamber lined with bones. Var did not investigate them closely; he knew their source. If he did not succeed in his mission, Soli's bones would be added to the collection. He went on.

The next chamber had several dry skulls. The third was mixed. There was no present sign of Minos.

It occurred to Var that the beast-god could go out and attack Soli while he searched the empty caverns. Hastily he retreated toward the entrance, passing through the skull chamber and an empty one.

And realized that he was lost in the labyrinth. He had missed a passage and now did not know where he was or in what direction lay the entrance. His wilderness-exploring sense, normally an automatic guide to such things, had let him down in this moment of preoccupation.

He could find his way out. He could sniff out his own spoor, or, failing that, make lines of bones to show his route, eliminating one false exit after another. But this would take time, and Soli might be in danger this moment. So he acted more directly.

"Minos!" he bawled. "Come fight me!"

"Must I?" a gentle voice replied behind him.

Var whirled. A man stood in one of the passages.

No—not a man. The body was that of a giant warrior, but the head was wooley and horned. No mere beard accounted for the effect. The front of the face pushed out in a solid snout, and the horns sprouted from just above the ears. It was as though the head of a bull had been grafted onto the body of a man. And the feet were hoofs, not blunted toes like Var's own, but solid round bovine hoofs. The teeth, however, were not herbivorous; they were pointed like those of a hound.

This was Minos.

Var had seen oddities before and had been expecting something of the sort. He made a motion with one stick, the excitement of battle growing within him. He supposed this was what some called fear.

"What brings you here by day, Var the Stick?" the god inquired quietly. "Always before you have come in darkness and never to my domicile."

"I came to fight," Var repeated. No one had told him the god could speak, or that he knew so much. How had Minos learned Var's name?

"Of course. But why at this moment? I have a busy day ahead. Yesterday I could have entertained you at greater leisure."

"It is Soli out there. My friend. For the sacrifice. I have sworn to kill the man—or beast or god—who harms her. But I would not wait to have her harmed."

Minos nodded, his woolly locks shaking. "You have fidelity and courage. But do you really believe you can kill me?"

"No. But I must try, for I have no life without Soli."

"Come. We can settle this without unpleasantness." Minos turned his broad back and trod down the passage, his horny feet clicking on the stone.

Var, nonplussed, followed.

They came to a larger chamber, in whose center was a boulder. "I lift this for exercise," Minos said. "Like this." He bent to grapple the stone, seemingly not concerned that an armed enemy stood behind him. Muscles bulged hugely all along his arms and sides and back. Var had not seen might like that since training with the Master.

The stone came up. Minos lifted it to chest height, held it there a few seconds, then eased it down. "Have to watch how you let go these monsters." He panted.

He stood back. "Now your turn. If you can hoist it, you may be a match for me."

Var hung his sticks at his belt and approached the rock. The god had trusted him, and he was obligated to extend trust in return.

He strained and hauled to no avail. He could not budge it. The thing would not even roll.

He gave up. "You're right. I am not as strong as you. But I might beat you in combat."

"Certainly," Minos said genially. His face was strange when he spoke, because he had to stretch his mouth closed around the muzzle and form the words with part of it. Even so, his enunciation was odd. "And we shall fight if you insist. But let us converse a time first. I seldom have opportunity to chat with an honest man."

Var was amenable. As long as the god was with him, Soli was safe. He wondered what would have happened had he attacked Minos while the god lifted the rock. That boulder might have come flying at him. . . .

They sat on crude chairs fashioned of bone tied with tendon, in another chamber. "Have a bite to eat," Minos said. "I have nuts, berries, bread—and meat, of course. But you know where that comes from."

Var knew. But the notion was not as shocking to him as he knew it was to others, for he had eaten many things in his wild childhood state. "I will share your food."

Minos reached into a pit and drew out a meaty rib. "I roasted these yesterday, so they remain wholesome," he explained, handing it to Var. He lifted a second for himself.

Var gnawed the rib, finding it far more tasty than raw rat meat. He wondered to which maiden it had belonged. Probably the last one; she had cried endlessly as they staked her out, and hadn't been very pretty. A bit fat, as this morsel verified. Momentarily queasy, Var washed his first mouthful down with the tepid water Minos provided.

"Where do you originate?" the god inquired.

Var explained about the circle culture.

"I have heard of it," Minos said. "But I must confess I thought it a myth, a fabrication, no offense intended. Now I see that it is a marvelous land indeed. But why did you and the girl depart?"

Var explained that too. It was remarkably easy to talk to this enemy giant and not entirely because of the stay it granted Soli.

Minos listened patiently to the whole tale. He was silent for a time when Var had finished. Then he said, "Is it possible—I am postulating from ignorance, understand—that the Nameless One is in fact her father?"

Var sat and chewed the maiden-meat, and diverse things began to fall into place in his mind, as though bees were settling into a hive. *The Master thought Var had slain his natural daughter!*

"Ironic," Minos said, "If that is the case. But the solution is simple. You have merely to show her to him when next you meet."

"Except—"

"Unfortunately, yes."

"Do you have to eat her?" It was hard to believe that so affable and reasonable a creature could balk on this point.

Minos sighed. "I am a god. Gods do not follow the conventions of man, by definition. I wish it were otherwise."

"But surely you have enough meat here to last another month?"

"I do not, for it spoils and I am not a ghoul. Some day I must require them to install refrigeration equipment. But that is not the problem. It is not primarily for the meat that I take the sacrifices."

Var chewed, not understanding.

"The flesh is only an incidental product," Minos said. "I use it because it is handy and I dislike waste. I make the best of the situation foisted on me by the temple."

"The temple makes you do this?"

"All temples, all religions, make their gods perform similarly. So it has always been, even before the Blast. The New Crete priests pretend that they serve Minos, but Minos serves them. It is a method of population control, in part, for the birthrate is governed by the percentage of nubile girls in the population. But mostly it is a way to retain power that would otherwise drift with the winds of politics and time. The common people have an abiding fear of me. I lurk near the bedstead of every disobedient child, I breathe misfortune on every tax evader. Yet I am single and mortal. The temple produced me by mutation and operation——"

"Like the Master!" Var exclaimed.

"So it seems. I should like to meet that man some day. You will note that I have stayed well within my domicile. Should I go near enough to the entrance, I should immediately lose control of myself. That is the way I have been designed; it is in my blood, in my brain."

This seemed remarkable to Var, but no more so than other things he had seen and learned in his travels. "What happens if a mistake is made, if the sacrifice is not chaste?"

Minos smiled hideously, all his teeth exposed on one side. "Why then I betake myself to the temple and I raise a fuss. And it is said that bad luck follows for a month."

The audience was over. "I must fight you," Var said.

"Surely you know I would kill you. I should think you would find a more romantic solution, pun intended. I would not like to have the blood of both of you on my horns, not when you have traveled so far and worked so hard and suffered such ironies already. Particularly when it is so easily avoided."

Var looked at him, not understanding. "She won't go with me. Not until the sacrifice."

Minos stood up. "There are things a god does not tell a man. Go now, or assuredly we *shall* fight, for the need is rising in me."

Var drew his sticks.

Minos knocked them numbingly from his hands with one lightning swipe. "Go! I will not reason with a fool."

Var, seeing that it was hopeless, picked up his sticks and went. This time he found the proper passage.

CHAPTER 17

Soli remained at the rock. Var ran to her. "You must go with me. Minos is coming!"

She hardly seemed surprised to see him alive. "I know. It is nearly noon." Her fair face was reddening in the slanting sun, and her lips were cracked.

"He doesn't want to kill you! But he has to if he finds you here."

"Yes." She was crying again, but he could tell from her expression that she had not changed her mind.

"I can't stop him. I'll try, but he will kill us both."

"Then go!" she screamed at him explosively. "I did this to save your stupid life. Why throw it away?"

"*Why?*" he screamed back. "I would rather die than have you die! You gave me nothing!"

She glared at him, abruptly calm. "Sosa told me all men were fools."

Var didn't see the relevance. But before he could speak again, there was a bellow from the labyrinth.

"Minos!" she whispered, terrified. "Oh, Var—please, please, *please* go! It's too late for me now."

The shape of the giant loomed at the cave entrance. Vapor snorted from the god's nostrils.

Var threw himself on Soli as though to shield her from the onslaught of the god, knowing this to be futile but determined not to desert her. He held her close and tight though she fought him, tearing his clothing with her feet and teeth. Finally he got her body pinned firmly against the wall so that her legs split and kicked behind him ineffectively while she hung by the manacles. "I will not leave you." He panted in her tangled hair.

Then her resistance collapsed. "Oh, Var, I'm sorry!" she sobbed. "I love you, you idiot."

There was no time to be amazed. He kissed her savagely, hearing the tramp of Minos' hoofs, the blast of Minos' breath.

Desperately they embraced, experiencing what had been building for three years, compressing it all into these last moments. Sharing their love absolutely, exquisitely, painfully.

And Minos came, and stopped, and paused, and made a noise half fury and half laughter, and passed on.

Only then did Var realize what had happened. What Minos had tried, subtly, to suggest to him.

He had indeed been a fool. Almost.

There were screams from the temple as Var yanked and pried and banged at the manacles still pinning Soli's bruised wrists against the stone. If he could get even one prong out her hand would be free, but the stone and metal were too strong.

He found a corroded spike in the dirt just beyond the canyon and wedged it under one bond and pounded it with a stone. And finally, reluctantly, one prong pulled out. But his spike snapped as he pried up and was useless for the other manacle.

The furor at the temple subsided. After an interval Minos came back, carrying two bodies. Var and Soli waited apprehensively.

The god halted. "This one's the high priestess," he remarked with satisfaction. "She deserves this, if anyone does. Poetic justice." He looked at Soli, who averted her face.

Minos reached forth with the hand thus freed and grasped the stubborn manacle. The muscles of that great arm twitched. The metal popped out of the wall with a spray of stone and fell to the ground. Soli was free.

Then the god fished a small package from his torn clothing and gave it to Soli, forcing it into her reluctant hand. "A gift," he said. "There never was anything personal about this, but I'm glad you became ineligible."

Soli did not answer, but she held onto the package. Minos took back the second corpse and marched into his labyrinth, humming a merry tune. He had reason to be happy: he would eat well this month.

"We'd better get out of here before the temple recovers," Var said. "Come on." He took Soli's hand and led her away.

Once they were in the forest he took off his tattered shirt

and put it about her. It formed into a short, baggy, but rather attractive dress, for her exposed legs were firm, her torso slender, and her face, despite the sunburn, lovely.

Soli, mutely curious, opened the package Minos had given her. It contained two keys and a paper with writing on it. She stared.

"What good are keys?" Var demanded. "We have no house."

"They belong to a powerboat," she said, reading the paper.

There were sea charts aboard the craft and voluminous tanks of gasoline and fresh water and canned goods. How Minos had arranged this they could not guess, but the boat had obviously been ready long before the two of them had entered the picture. Perhaps he had intended to escape himself but had given up the notion because of his biological urgencies. Or maybe he was less a slave to the temple than he had admitted. He could have many luxurious boats tucked away. . . .

From the maps they learned that they were far south of where they had supposed. The tunnel to China—actually, to Siberia—left from farther along. They had taken the Aleutian series, which led nowhere. However, with this stout craft it should be possible to make the crossing, following the island chain to the Kamchatka peninsula. From there they could either trek overland north and west and south around the Sea of Okhotsk or continue island hopping directly southwest toward Japan.

Var's head spun with the unfamiliar names Soli pieced out. This weird map was like the Master's books: It predated the Blast and so contained much nonsense. Some of the islands might not be there any more.

Somehow neither person suggested that they go back past the amazon hive, on to Alaska, north to the true crossing. Or even back to America. China had become a fixed objective, for no good reason now. Obviously they were not going to be satisfied with anyone's culture but their own. And if the Master were still on their trail, he should have caught up by this time.

They could go home, and Soli could rejoin whichever father she chose, and Var could be a warrior again, and their relationship would be over. They would never need to see each other again. Yet they continued west.

A storm blew up, and they hastily docked the boat on the shore of a deserted islet. Then fair weather, and they moved through deep water at top speed, letting the fine engine do the work.

In time, the entire New Crete residence of two years tended to encyst itself as a thing apart, an unreal memory. Soli became the child again, Var the ugly warrior. They were not ready for love. They were two people united by a common purpose and an unspoken affection.

This was, at any rate, the way Var saw it, though he did not work it out neatly or consciously. More than once he observed Soli staring at his bracelet. Perhaps she was remembering the way she had preserved it for him, at the near sacrifice of her own life. He was sorry that he had told her this was foolish, for that must have hurt her feelings—but it was true. Had the bracelet been sold, they need never have suffered those two years on New Crete.

That reminded him circularly of another point, the one Minos had made. *Could* the Master be Soli's natural father? Now this seemed less reasonable than it had in the cave, and Var could not bring himself to present the notion openly. How would Soli react, having the paternity of Sol questioned? She loved Sol dearly and hardly knew the Master. And if it *were* true, how would the Master react, knowing that Var had lied to him, making him believe his daughter had been slain?

The wide expanse of the sea went on and on, hypnotic, beautiful, boring. The sparse islands were barren and did not conform exactly to the indications of the map. They took turns steering, following a marking on the compass, a dial that always pointed north. The sun and the stars also served, and whenever they encounted a feature recognizable on the map they corrected course accordingly.

And a few days after they thought the ocean would never end, they sighted the mainland of Asia.

And the people spoke incomprehensibly.

"Yes, of course," Soli said in response to his bewilderment. "They speak Chinese. Or they will, when we reach China. The map says it's—well, see, we have a long way to go yet."

Two thousand miles or more, it seemed to Var. Months of travel.

They were sick of the ocean, but the overland route looked worse. They searched out a place to buy gasoline, paying for it with artifacts from the boat, and hopped southwest along what the map called the Kuril islands, then north inside of Sakhalin, and finally back to the mainland of Manchuria. The preposterous pre-Blast names were fascinating.

Now the land route promised to be more direct and safe. They had either to use the boat or dispose of it, and they remained more at home afoot. So, regretfully, they decided to sell it. They went to a place that had similar craft and inquired until an old man was brought who spoke a little American.

"America?" he asked, amazed. "Destroyed—Blast."

By and by they conducted a party to the boat, and the sale was completed. Soli was cynical about the value, expecting to be cheated, but there seemed to be little choice. At any rate, they obtained enough currency to buy local outfits and equipment and some written primers in the language, including an ancient pre-Blast text with American equivalents.

They hiked again and drilled each other on the written symbols. Soli said they were not like the writing she knew but that they made sense once she got used to them. And though there were many spoken dialects, so that travelers like them would be constantly confused, the written language covered the entire region. With these symbols, they could always communicate, provided they met someone literate.

Overall, the landscape resembled what they had known on the other continent, mountainous, wild and riddled by patches of badlands radiation. The natives near the coast were civilized in the fashion of New Crete, without human sacrifice, but with other cultural problems. Those inland were more primitive, like the American nomads, but without the substantial benefits of crazy technology or supplied hostels. Most left the strangers alone, but some were belligerent, and no circle circumscribed the combat. Had Var and Soli not been apt at self-defense they would not have lived very long.

They followed the river Amur inland, not from any love of the water but because it showed the best route through the formidable mountain ranges. When it veered northwest, they shifted to a large tributary. Months passed, and they came at last to the fringe of the actual Chinese territories. The Chinese influence, like that of the crazies in America, extended through the entire region, perhaps all the continent;

their written language unified the divers peoples in a subtle but comprehensive way. Var, having learned the very real constraints upon the seemingly free nomad society, was sure that similar factors operated here. Similar in principle, if not in detail. There must, indeed, be a Chinese Helicon.

Yet as they neared their supposed destination, their camaraderie became more strained. Soli was filling out and Var was too well aware of this. Sometimes he touched his bracelet, thinking of offering it to her; but this always reminded him of what had happened when he first took his manhood. Girls of band-borrowing age did not appreciate ugly men, and Var knew himself to be grotesque.

And she was beautiful. Perhaps in the flower of her maidenhood her mother Sola had been like this, so lovely that the mightiest warriors of the age contested for her favor and lived lies without complaint.

Soli had never remarked on it, but she could hardly favor his mottled skin, battered countenance and clubbed extremities. Children did not care so much about such things, but Soli would never be a child again.

Var occasionally saw, the literate ladies of this core-Chinese culture. They were like crafted dolls, delicate and delightful, their motions constrained, their demeanors diffident. In contrast, the peasant women were brutes, stout, plain, hunched of body, course of expression.

Var knew that the wandering life he was making for Soli would shape her into the peasant mold. He could not bear the thought. Increasingly it preyed upon him, and when he saw some crone he fancied Soli's face on her.

The background level of civilization rose as they entered the Chinese heartland. The people here were yellowish of skin and their eyes were different, and their manners tended to be almost ritualistically polite. The women were eloquent, the highborn ones. Var learned that they attended institutions somewhat like the crazy schools that brought them to the mature state. Then, as sophisticated ladies, they married and did not do hand labor again. Household servants performed the chores.

Var decided that this would be a better life for Soli. But he didn't know how to explain this philosophy, and feared she would not understand his intent, so he didn't try.

One night when she slept beside him in the forest, he rose stealthily. She woke, however. "Var?"

"Have to—you know," he said, feeling a pang of guilt for his lie. To reassure her, he urinated noisily against a tree, then squatted. In a moment her breathing became even, and he moved quietly away.

Just as he passed beyond the normal hearing range, he heard something, either an animal moving, or Soli rolling over and striking dry leaves. His pang came again, quite forcefully, and he wavered and almost went back. But he heard nothing else and forced himself to go on.

He ran five miles back to one of the schools they had passed that day. He pounded on the gate for admittance and finally roused an old caretaker, a nearsighted, gray-bearded, bony man who was not pleased to be disturbed at this hour. Var tried to talk to him, but his words were evidently of the wrong dialect and inadequate to the concept. He did make the oldster understand that he had to see the authority figure for the school. With grumbling, the man retired into the bowels of the building to search that person out, while Var waited nervously outside the gate.

Ten minutes later he was admitted to the presence of the head matron. She had obviously just gotten up and wore a nightrobe, but he could tell from her aspect that she was sharp of mind. Her face was lined though she was heavy-set, and her hair was glossy black.

She could not understand him either, though she appeared to speak a number of dialects. Then she made a symbol on a sheet of paper, and Var knew they could communicate after all. For these symbols were universal here and had the same meaning regardless of the dialect spoken, or even the language. Var was borderline-literate now, so far as these symbols were concerned; he had picked up several hundred in the past few months, as had Soli, and could use them for making purchases and clarifying posted directives such as "Radiation Ahead."

For two hours they passed messages back and forth. At the end of that silent dialogue Var had purchased admittance for Soli to the school. He was to pay the tuition by doing brutework for the maintenance department.

He described her location and a party went out, armed. Var reported to the cellar, where the gray-bearded man showed him to a wooden bunk near the giant furnace. He was now the assistant to this man, for good or ill.

He had sold them both into a kind of servitude. But Soli would emerge with her future secure.

It was a month before he saw her again, for the hired help had no legitimate contact with the elite girls. But as he hauled wood and peat for the furnace, and pounded stakes for new fencing and carried supplies for the daily wagon to the kitchen and did the thousand things the older man had somehow managed before, he picked up hints. He mastered the common local words and received the local gossip.

They had brought in a spitfire that night. A wild country urchin who struck out with sticks as devastatingly as a seasoned fighting man. They had threatened her with guns, but she had not yielded, and they had not dared to use them because she was supposed to be captured and trained as a lady. They had finally subdued her with a net, after suffering several casualties.

Soli! Soli! Var ached with her misery, ashamed to have brought this on her. How could she know that it was for the best, that she might spend the rest of her life at leisure?

The old man shook his head. He could not understand why they should want to train a wild peasant and an outlander at that, for she was fair of skin and round of eye. But rather attractive, he confessed, once subdued and cleaned up.

Var realized that the man made no connection between him and Soli. This once, his discoloration had worked to his advantage. He wanted to watch, to be sure the terms of the bargain were fulfilled, but not to associate with her, for that would hurt her manufactured image. She was to be a lady; he could never be a gentleman.

Then he was cutting back shrubbery beside the wall, and she was taken for a walk inside the grounds. He saw her with a matron and three other girls, dressed in chaste gowns. He was reminded horribly of her stay in New Crete, waiting for the sacrifice. Then, as now, he had been the instrument that confined her. The whole thing suddenly seemed so similar that he longed to grab her and run for the forest and undo what he had done.

He averted his face, afraid of the consequence if she should see him now.

The little party walked along the flowered pathway, treading in step to the murmured cadence of the matron. Each girl took tiny steps. Var heard the petite patter, aware of their motions peripherally. They were learning to walk like ladies, daintily, intriguingly.

Var continued clipping, his back to the walk. The girls passed so close he could smell their fragrance. They did not stop. After a while they were guided inside, and Var was both relieved and saddened. It would have been folly to speak to Soli, but the urge had been almost unbearably strong.

Regret it as he might, he knew that the school was honoring the agreement they had made. He could not be the first to break it.

That night, as the oldster lay in the heat ready to sleep, a hooded visitor came to the cellar. The old man went to investigate, was given something and stood aside. The figure came to stand over Var's bunk.

Jarred out of his reverie, Var looked up.

It was Soli. Her eyes were luminous under the hood. "You did it," she said softly.

Var just looked at her, struck by the beauty of her features. Already the training had had its impact on her bearing, and the cosmetics had enhanced her splendor.

"I saw you in the garden," she murmured, continuing to look down on him with an expression he did not understand.

Then her hand came from under the cloak, holding a slipper. Down it came against his stomach, stingingly.

"I thought you were dead!" she cried, and now he recognized her emotion: fury. Then she turned and left.

She had thought him dead. He had never suspected that, but in retrospect it was obvious. Attacked in the night, captured, hauled away to a strange institution without sight of him—what would her natural interpretation have been except that he had been killed in the same fracas? So she had resigned herself . . . and discovered suddenly that it was a lie.

Why had he meddled? He had never intended to have it come out that way.

The old man returned, chuckling. Obviously he had now made the connection between the spitfire and the handyman. Would he keep the confidence? It didn't matter, since the arrangement was legitimate and Soli knew the truth.

Var lay awake a long time, not certain whether to be pleased or saddened by Soli's attitude. The sudden sight of her had been a shocking stimulus. So lovely, so angry! Did she hate him for deceiving her? Or would she recognize

the advantage he had arranged for her? Surely she could
see that they could not have wandered endlessly across the
continents of the world. A beautiful girl and an ugly man.
Such a life would not hurt him, of course, for he had no
higher potential; indeed, it would be easy for him to revert
to the wild state and range the badlands. But Soli—Soli
could be a lady, graceful and cultured. He owed it to her
to make that life possible.

He still felt guilty. He still longed for her free companion-
ship, as it had been in the early days before New Crete.
It was impossible, for she would never be young again,
but still he wished, and suffered.

Two weeks later, as he gathered fallen wood in the forest
and loaded it on a hand wagon for hauling, she came to
him again. This time she was dressed in boy's clothes, with
her hair concealed and artful smudges on her face. She
looked like a marauding urchin, a guise she had long been
versed in, as he knew.

"I'm running away," she said. "Come with me, as you
used to."

Var grabbed her and carried her back toward the school
enclosure. She could have disabled him in a number of ways,
but she offered only token resistance.

"I know you're paying for me," she said. "I hate you."

He knew she didn't mean it, but the words stung just
the same.

"Why do you want me here?" she asked pitifully. "Why
can't we tour the countryside together? That's all I want."

Var shifted his grip and continued carrying. She was lithe
in his arms, all curve and tension.

She drew her head up and kissed him on the lips, as
a woman might. As Sola, her mother, had. "Just to be with
you, Var."

Temptation smote him savagely. It was the child he remembered, but the woman had hold on his longing too. Yet
he walked, unanswering.

"Do you want me to cry?" But she didn't cry, though
it would have broken him. And when he didn't answer, she
murmured: "I'm sorry I hit you with my slipper." And then,
when they came in sight of the buildings: "It should have
been a *star!*"

And had she *had* a morningstar mace, he reflected, she

might very well have bashed him with it, such was her momentary fury.

He turned her over to a matron. As he tromped dejectedly back to the forest he heard her beginning screams, part agony, part rage. They were beating her for the infraction. The instrument was padded, so as not to leave any disfiguring mark, but he knew it hurt. And they both had known the penalty. The matron had made that clear at the outset: Discipline was her watchword.

But Soli, veteran of stick combat, could not be made to scream through pain. She was merely letting Var know and satisfying the matron, who of course was not fooled. The ritual had to be complete, lest the other girls grow similarly willful.

Var was given one day off in every ten, though he was willing to work. The head matron, fair-minded, insisted on this too. There was a town nearby, and his second holiday he went there to look about. But he was not comfortable and a number of the natives treated him with subtle disrespect, not desiring his company. It was so hard to know when to smile and when to react, when no circle marked the boundary between courtesy and combat. Once a young rowdy laid a hand on him and Var struck him to the ground, but it changed nothing.

No, for him the badlands were best. He understood neither this culture nor the American nomad culture, and was better off alone. Once he had seen Soli through the training, he would doff civilization of any type and become completely, happily wild.

But he remembered Soli and knew that he was deceiving himself. He would never be happy without her, child or woman.

CHAPTER 18

"I have found out whose men have been assembling here the past month," the oldster said.

In the course of nearly a year Var had learned to converse with him, though he had never had occasion to learn his name. The man was always full of gossip, and Var was not interested. He had observed the troops and known them to be the advance guard for some royal personage. Most of the girls of the school were highborn, and it was a mark of distinction to graduate and depart in style with an armed retinue, even if one had to be hired for the purpose. Often the men assembled in advance, waiting for their masters to appear, so that as the end of term approached the school grounds resembled a battle camp. Var had jousted familiarly with some, showing off his ability with the sticks. But most were armed with handguns.

"The ones in gold livery," the oldster said, perceiving the waning attention of his limited audience. "Who speak to no one and drill on a private field."

Those were intriguing. No one seemed to know which lord they served or what girl would be honored by them, but over a score were present, in beautifully matched uniforms. And they were crack troops; Var had covertly observed their practice maneuvers and firing.

Seeing that he had Var's interest at last, the oldster continued: "They serve the Emperor Ch'in. He must have chosen another bride."

Var was impressed. Ch'in controlled the largest of the rival kingdoms of the south, and through political intrigue and judicious force of arms had expanded his sphere of influence considerably in the last generation. Just as the Master had controlled an empire in America, this man had built one here in China, though it was not as large as the Master's and did not extend into the region this school was located in. He had at least thirty wives already, but was always on the lookout for attractive girls or politically expedient unions. Evidently his eye had fallen on one of these here, and he intended to see that nothing happened to her before he arrived.

But none of that concerned Var. He hoped to see Soli graduated and placed in some prosperous household, after which he could retreat to the badlands. He would regret never seeing her again, regret it intensely, but this was the hard choice he had made when he brought her to the school. She would, in time, be happy, and that was what was most important. Her childhood was behind her, and he was part of that childhood.

The head matron summoned him. "I have excellent news for you," she said, studying him in a way that hinted at a dark side to that news. "We have found a placement for your ward."

The information crushed him. Suddenly he realized what the matron had probably known all along: that he didn't want Soli placed. He couldn't voluntarily give her up when that moment came, despite all his plans and pretensions.

"That *is* what you required," she reminded him gently.

"Yes." He felt numb.

"And as is customary in such cases, her tuition will be refunded. We shall return it to you in lieu of your wages this past year. You will find it to be a comfortable amount."

Var followed this with difficulty. "You aren't charging for her training?"

"Certainly we're charging! We are not a charitable institution. But another party has undertaken to cover it. So it is no longer necessary for you to do so, though we have been well satisfied with your contribution. We shall be owing you money, as I said, at graduation."

"Who—why—?"

"The lord who is to marry her, of course." Again that intent look. "We're rather pleased with this placement; it is an auspicious one."

"Ch'in!" he cried, making the connection.

"He prefers anonymity prior to the ceremony," she said. "That is why I did not mention it to you before. But you

do deserve to know, and with his livery so evident. . . .
He desired a foreign bride, being momentarily sated with
domestic affairs."

Her nicety of expression was wasted on him. "But Ch'in!"

"Isn't this what you said you wanted? The highest possible
placement for your ward, that she should never again be
in want, never again run with a savage?" Once more that
obscure glance.

Yes, it was what he had wanted. What he had *thought*
he had wanted, once. The matron had more than fulfilled the
bargain. He could not back out of it now.

"It is not necessary for you to be separated from her,"
she continued with a certain wise compassion. "The Emperor
Ch'in is always in the market for strong men-at-arms, and
he seldom pays close attention to a wife for more than a
year. His earlier wives have considerable freedom provided
they are circumspect."

Var had once been naïve about such things, but he had
learned from experience. In this land, the appearance was
often more important than the reality, as it was in America,
too. She was suggesting to him that he take service with the
emperor now and make his overtures to Soli after a year
or so, when she might have borne a child to Ch'in and when
some newer bride would command Ch'in's attention. Such arrangements were common, and the emperor, though cogni-
zant, did not object—so long as no public issue was made.
Soli could have a royal life, and Var could have Soli, if
he were patient and discreet.

The matron had showed him the expedient course. He
thanked her and left. But he was *not* satisfied, and expedience
had seldom appealed to him before. Suddenly the thought of
Soli rolling in the arms of a stout Chinese emperor repelled
him. He had never thought it through to this point, to realize
that she would buy her luxury with her body, as surely as
he had bought her training with his own body. He was
furiously jealous of the suitor he had never seen and whom
Soli had never seen.

He remembered Soli's insistence that she did not favor
the schooling and only wanted to travel with him. Now,
suddenly, this loomed far more importantly. Now that she
could marry richly would she feel the same?

It became imperative that he ask her.

But of course he could not simply walk into the school

dormitory and put the question to her there. There were strict
regulations. She would be beaten if she were caught speaking to him, just as any girl was beaten who disobeyed any
school rule, however minor. But this late in the term they
were supposed to discipline themselves, and increasing social
stigmata attached to infractions. Soli, a foreigner, had become quite as sensitive to this as any native. So Var approached cautiously. She would speak to him if he were
circumspect: that is, if they were not caught.

And he discovered that the emperor's men were on the
job. Every approach to Soli's dormitory was subtly guarded.

Var, not to be put off by mere physical barriers, picked
the weakest section of the defense and moved through. This
was the garden behind her second-floor window. He intended only to knock the lone sentry out with one blow
from one stick, but the man was alert and escaped the blow,
and fired his pistol. Var brought him down, but roughly,
and there was no chance to scale the wall before reinforce-
ments came.

They were well organized, and they had rifles. A semi-
circle of uniformed men closed in, pinning him in a shrinking
area beside the wall. A vehicle crashed through the bushes,
making him wince because he had carefully tended those
plants. A light speared from it, catching him.

Var stood still, knowing he was trapped. He had not
suspected that they would act so competently. He could not
make a break against lights and guns.

"Who is it?" a voice called from the truck.

"A maintenance worker," another replied. "I've seen him
around."

"What is he doing here?"

"He cuts the hedges."

"At *night?*"

"What are you doing here, laborer?" This was directed
at Var.

"I have to talk to . . . a girl," he said, realizing that
he was hurting himself by his directness.

"*Which* girl?"

"Soli."

There was a huddle behind the light. Var remembered that
they had renamed Soli for school purposes in the interest
of minimizing her vulgar origin. The name he had used

was not familiar to them, and he could avoid the truth even now. "The one you guard, betrothed to Ch'in."

"Bring him to the barracks," the officer snapped.

They brought him. "What do you want of this girl?" the officer demanded in the privacy of the temporary building the soldiers used.

"To take her away, if she wants to come." The truth comforted him in the telling, despite the effect it had on these men. He *did* want Soli, even though it might cost her luxury. He knew that now.

"Do you understand that we shall kill anyone who tries such a thing?"

"Yes."

The officer paused, thinking him a fool or a simpleton. "You struck down the sentry?"

"Yes."

"Why do you want to take this particular girl?"

"I love her."

"Why do you think she might go with you, an ugly hunch-back, when the pinnacle is within her reach by staying?"

"I brought her."

"You knew her before?"

"For four years we traveled together."

"Fetch the matron," the officer said to one of the men. "Heat the knife," he said to another. And to Var: "If she denies your story, you shall die as an example to those who would thwart Ch'in. If she confirms it, you will merely lose your interest in this girl. In any girl."

Var watched the knife being turned over and over in the flame of a great candle and pondered how many he could kill before that blade touched him.

The matron came. "It is true," she said. "He brought her and has paid for her keep by his labors and kept her here when she wanted to escape. It is his right to take her away again, if she wishes to accompany him."

"It *was* his right," the officer said grimly, "until the Emperor Ch'in selected her for his retinue. No other rights exist."

She faced him without alarm. "We are not in Ch'in's demesne."

"You may readily be added to it, madam."

She shrugged. "A strike into this region at this time would unite the enemies of Ch'in in the north, at a time when his main force is occupied to the south. Is one bride worth it?"

The officer pondered, taken aback by the political acumen of the matron. "The Emperor does not wish bloodshed to mar his wedding day. We shall pay this man a fair price for his prior claim and deport him unharmed from the vicinity. Should he return before the nuptial, he will be held until that day is passed, then suffer the death of a thousand cuts." He fetched a bag of coins. "This will cover it."

The matron looked at Var soberly. "His compromise is reasonable. Accept it, nomad. And take this too." She handed him a packet.

Var was reminded of the manner of Minos, god of New Crete, as he gave Soli the keys to the powerboat. He realized that in some subtle manner she was helping him. He could either start fighting now—sure death, however many he took with him—or trust her guidance and acquiesce to the officer's terms.

He accepted the money and the package and accompanied the guards to their truck. He had not given up, but this did seem to be the best present course.

Six hours later he was set down, alone, a hundred miles to the north. Dawn was breaking over the badlands.

The packet contained a map and a human thumb.

The map was routine, covering all this region. Except for a single location marked in red. The thumb—

Var was familiar with digits, since his own were misshapen. He could recognize certain men as readily by their hands as by their faces. This was not a Chinese digit; it was American. Massive, with fine mesh under the skin, scarred.

This was the Master's thumb.

Obviously the matron knew where the Master was, alive or dead, and had known for some time. She must then also know the connection between Var and Soli and the Nameless One. Now she had chosen to reveal her information to Var. Why?

He shook his head, not comprehending that part of it. She was an honest woman but, like so many of these people, mysterious in her ways.

He had less than a fortnight to recover Soli, if he intended to do so before Ch'in took her to his couch. If he wanted to present her with a fair choice between the ugly nomad and the rich powerful emperor.

He could return to the school in time, for they had under-estimated his capacity for walking. But he knew the officer had not been bluffing about the fate that awaited him there. And suddenly he was unsure what Soli's reaction would be. She *had* been angry with him, and she *could* have a luxurious life. . . .

He could get to the indicated spot on the map in a week's strenuous marching. Surely the Master's thumb had come from there. It was time for him to settle his dif-ference with his longtime friend and mentor—or to know for certain that it could never be settled. If the great man were dead. . . .

It was an arena. Gladiators met each other and wild animals in mortal combat, for the delight of paying specta-tors. The star attraction was a pair of foreign savages, prisoners captured half a year before by troops of a lesser kingdom in a border skirmish. Sol and the Master, of course.

Brief inquiry enabled Var to come at some semblance of the truth. The two had followed Var into the Aleutian tunnel but, more canny than he, had avoided the menace of the automatic sweeper. They had fought off the amazons but had been balked by the radiation at the bridge. So they had taken the long way round, knowing that Var would not stop until he reached the mainland across the ocean. Back through the tunnel, overland north to the true transpacific tunnel and down the Asiatic coast. They had traversed a lot of territory, fighting off enemies of animate and inanimate types, and had taken years in the process. Then they had run afoul of one border patrol too many—actually a quasi-official bandit band—and had been taken under the threat of massed rifles.

After their wounds had healed, the two had been sold to the arena. Their left thumbs had been cut off to mark their status. Now they were earning out their contracts, at fees that would necessitate a decade to meet the price.

"I will pay off the contract," Var said. He put the bag of coins into the hand of the agent at the gate.

The man counted the money and nodded. "Ch'in currency. Very strong. For which one?"

Var described the Master.

"Very well." Var had expected haggling, for his little bag

could hardly be worth a ten-year contract. The man gave him a receipt written in the Chinese symbols. Var took it eagerly and entered the grounds, finding his way toward the gladiators' accommodations. It had been surprisingly easy.

But he had a second thought and paused to puzzle out the symbols. The note was phony; it granted admission to the grounds and nothing else. He had been cheated.

Angry, he started back but soon realized that the man would have hidden the money and perhaps disappeared himself, after this illicit haul. No one else would choose to believe Var's complaint. Arenas were known to be dens of vice and corruption; he should have been alert.

Still, they had set the pattern, meeting his honest if naïve approach with dishonesty. Var's ethics of civilization were not fundamentally ingrained, for he had come by them only through his contact with the Master and had not had them reinforced by his adventures beyond America. He treated other men as they treated him, and he knew how to look out for himself, thus warned.

He threw away the paper and continued on to the gladiatorial pen. This was a high-wire stockade at whose corners wooden towers rose. A man with a rifle stood watch within each edifice, facing toward the center.

Nearby were the animal cages. Tigers, bison, snakes, vicious dogs and some mutants from the badlands. These were set up as a sideshow when not in use. From the healing wounds some had Var inferred that they were used repeatedly. Probably the gladiators were given a bonus for defeating an animal impressively without killing it.

He scouted the rest of the compound. This was an off day. The shows only took place every three or four afternoons. Relatively few sightseers like himself were about. In one side lot there were several trucks used for transporting animals and equipment from time to time. The show traveled every few months, seeking new pasture and new audience—and perhaps as a hedge against too great an accumulation of vengeance-minded suckers.

Satisfied, Var retreated to a comfortable wilderness patch and slept. He would be busy tonight.

At night, refreshed, Var re-entered the compound, using his well-practiced stealth. He pried down a window in a locked truck, got the door open, used pliers on the wiring in the manner he had learned as a handyman dealing with balky

equipment and unblocked the wheels. Then he moved to the
nearest guard tower, climbed it noiselessly and tapped the
rifleman on the head with a makeshift singlestick. He did
the same for the second tower, having learned from his
brief experience with Ch'in's men not to give a man with a
gun any chance to react. The section of fence between these
two points was partially out of sight of the far towers, so a
passage was clear. Var took metal clippers and made a hole.
He entered, carrying a handgun and flashlight taken from the
second guard.

The gladiators were in a locked shed that reeked of
excrement. Var used screwdriver and crowbar to unlock it
with minimum noise, working on the side away from the
manned towers. He knew the occupants would overhear but
would not give him away. They might, however, attempt to
overpower him and make their own escape. He had to be
ready.

He kicked open the door, shone the light inside and stood
back. "I have a gun," he said softly in the local dialect.
Then, in American: "Come out singly and make no sound—
if you want your freedom."

"Var the Stick!" the Master said at once, but low, for he
was well aware that they had to stay below the hearing
level of the tower guards. His bulk showed in the doorway.
"Do you bring a gun to meet me?"

That familiar voice sent a shiver through him, but Var
answered firmly. "No. This is not the circle. You swore to
kill me because you thought I had killed your daughter. I did
not kill her. I will take you to her now."

There was a long pause. "Not my daughter—*his*," the
Master said at last. And Sol appeared beside him, a somber
shape. "We suspected as much, when we had the description
of the boy you traveled with. But we didn't *know*, and you
kept running. So we had to follow."

So the entire chase had been for nothing! Var could have
taken Soli to the Master or even let Sol see her that time
they met in the circle, and the oath would have been voided.
It would not even have affected the contest for the mountain, because Bob had already reneged on that agreement.
Such irony!

Var looked up to discover the Master before him, well
within striking range. But of course the Weaponless would
not have struck outside the circle, not against one who

shared that convention. And had he wanted to violate the code, he could have thrown something. Except that his thumb was missing; that would have made it harder.

"I should have questioned you," the Nameless One said. "A day after you were gone, I knew I had acted wrongly, for you had done only what I sent you to do. It was the mountain Helicon that betrayed us both. Betrayed Sol too, for he did not know that his child had been sent until he learned that she was dead."

Var remembered that Soli had said her parents hadn't known, that Bob almost never told the truth and that she had cooperated because of Bob's threat against their lives. Ugly business—the underworld master's revenge for the nomad attack. "That's why he came, to avenge her?"

"To bury her. He had already avenged her when he slew Bob and fired Helicon. Sosa disappeared in that carnage. All that was left was to bury Soli, but he could not find her body. So he came, and by the time we met and worked it out, you were gone again, with your . . . sister."

They were wasting time. "Come with me," Var said. "She is in—in a school. There will be trouble."

It was as though there had never been strife between them. They came: the Master, Sol and four other gladiators of diverse and grotesque aspect. Var led them through the fence and past the animal cages, ready to loose the beasts upon the compound if any alarm were cried. But, almost disappointingly, there was no disturbance. They piled into the truck and Var started it, using the shorted wiring. They were off.

Emperor Ch'in had arrived, together with more of his retinue, by the time the truckful of gladiators nudged into the vicinity and parked surreptitiously near the school grounds. Uniformed troops were everywhere. A frontal attack would have been sheer folly. And they still were not sure how Soli would feel about it.

"She did not ask to attend the school?" the Master inquired. "She was satisfied to travel with you?"

"So she said," Var admitted. "A year ago. But she was growing up. . . ."

"Now she is grown—why should the situation be otherwise? Would you have her roam again?"

Terrible uncertainty smote him. "I don't know."

"This Ch'in, I have heard of him. Isn't that a good marriage?"

"Yes."

"But you don't want her to have it?"

Var became even more confused. "I want to talk to her. If she *wants* to marry Ch'in—"

The Master grunted. "We shall put her to the test."

They spent the night in the truck in the woods. The Chinese gladiators went after food and gasoline zestfully, enjoying this lark. The Master questioned Var on every aspect of his association with Soli, while Sol, eerily silent, listened. It occurred to Var that he did not know what was in the minds of these men. So far as Soli was concerned, their reactions were suspect. They might have no sympathy whatever with his blunted desires.

But he discovered that he had lost his independence of action since releasing these men. The Master dominated the entire group, and his intelligence radiated out almost tangibly. Var though he recognized in this man some of the qualities that made Soli what she was, that had, in fact, attracted him to her—yet the Master denied siring her. So things had been thrown into confusion again.

Var peered from the concealed truck while the others marched off to attend the graduation ceremony, his heart pounding. Eager to act, he was helpless, dependent on the motives of others, uncertain of his own.

CHAPTER 19

Soli slept fitfully. The events of her life passed through her mind, now that she faced a drastic change. She did not remember her early residence among the nomads, only snow and terrible cold, her father Sol protecting her though they both meant to die. Then somehow they were alive again, painfully so, and Sosa was her new mother. And after the shock of change, it had been good, for Sosa was a remarkable woman, at once devastating in combat and loving in person. And the underworld was fascinating. Until Bob had acquainted her with the brutality of politics and sent her out with her sticks to defend her way of life from the savages.

She had supposed all nomads to be mutilated. Var had had splotched skin and funny hands and a hunch in his back. Yet Sosa had taught her that appearance meant little in a man; that his endurance and skill in combat were more important, and his personality more important still. "If a man is strong and honest and kind—like your father—trust in him and make him your friend," had been her advice.

The men of the underworld had not met this simple set of standards. Jim the Librarian was honest and kind and intelligent, but not strong; a single blow to the gut would have put him in the infirmary. Bob the Leader was strong but neither honest nor kind. In fact, only her father Sol met Sosa's standards. So she learned the art of the sticks from him, and learned it well, and waited.

And ugly Var had been strong, if not as skilled with the sticks as she. And he had been honest, for he had not dropped rocks on her, though she would have dodged any that might have come. And he had been kind, for he had

157

protected her against the awful cold, even as her father had done before. That was the one enemy she could not face boldly: She hated and feared the cold.

So she had known him for a good man, though he was an enemy savage, and she had never been disappointed subsequently. Oh, he was not exactly smart, but neither was Sol. Men like Bob and the Nameless One were awesome, because their minds were more deadly than their bodies. She preferred an associate whose motives she could fathom.

At what point this appreciation had phased into love she was not certain. It had been a gradual thing, deepening with further association and ripening with her womanhood. But she tended to place the transition at the time she had been stung in the cold by the poisonous bug and he had carried her all the way back to the cabin and cared for her there. She had been conscious much of the time, but unable to move or respond. Thus she had observed him when he supposed himself effectively alone, and knew that he had fought for her long before he confessed as much.

She had decided then to take his golden bracelet when she was old enough to do so and to honor the full commitment the act implied. When she had learned that Sol was following them too, she had stayed with Var despite her ache to rejoin her father, knowing she would lose Var if she let him go on alone. Then he had saved her from the tunnel sweeper and from the vicious amazons and yet again from the radiation she could not detect for herself. And once more, in the boat, he had intercepted with his own body the arrows marked for her.

Five times he had preserved her life at peril to his own, asking nothing in return, not even her company unless freely given. He was quite a man, and not merely for his courage and sacrifice. If she had not loved him already, she would surely have done so then. But when she brought them to New Crete he had been dying. Then she had seen the manner she had to repay her debt to him. For a moment she had been tempted to cash in his golden bracelet, realizing its disproportionate value there; but that would have made it unavailable for her own subsequent possession and what went with it. And they might just have taken it as they took the boat, with no return favor. Though they both might die, she could not bring herself to give up that dream.

So it had had to be the temple, the one offering they

could not simply claim offhand, the one bargain she could
hold them to. She had cried; not so much for herself as for
her loss of him. She had known, via the temple grapevine,
that he had settled into a mundane task and she suffered
to imagine how that demeaned him while she thrilled to
believe that he missed her as she missed him. Sweet girlish
dreams, nonsensical but essential. She even fancied that he
watched her from time to time, romantically; that he might
even challenge the god Minos for her.

And then he *had* come, just when she was resigned to
her violent demise. And she had watched him go into the
labyrinth and condemned herself for her idealistic folly.

"If ever I see him again alive," she had sworn to herself
as she stood chained and helpless, "I shall clasp him to me
and tell him I love him." But it had been the abandoned
conviction of desperation.

Yet it had happened.

And somehow, from that moment, she had ceased to
understand him. She was woman now, ready and able to accept him as man, and the proof had been made. Still he
treated her as child. Why, when they had already made
spectacular love? Why did he withdraw when she approached? *Why had he stayed two years, retaining his bracelet, and come for her and taken her—only to ignore her
offerings now?*

She had gone along, powerless to change the situation.
And gradually she discovered that she had changed, not he,
and that he did not realize this. Not quite. Var was naïve.
He had begun his journey with a child, and in his mind he
still traveled with a child. In his eye, she would always be a
child.

Then, just as she was adjusting to that situation, a raiding
party had caught her unaware and brought her here. At
first she thought Var was dead; then she learned that he had
arranged it. Her fury had lasted for weeks.

Until it occurred to her that she could emerge from
this inane purgatory a woman, in his estimation. He wanted
her here so that he could officially accept the transition
that had already taken place. So that he could present her
his bracelet honorably.

That changed her attitude. She discovered that there was
a good education to be had here. The matrons were rigorous
but sincere, and they knew a great deal of value. Soli

perfected her reading ability in the symbols of this continent and mastered other disciplines she had hardly been aware existed. Most important, she became adept at female artistries that would twist and remold the impetus of almost any male. This, indeed, was as intricate a combat as any with weapons, and as potentially rewarding.

Var had some surprises coming.

Now she had been betrothed—against her will—to the Emperor Ch'in. It was an advantageous liaison, no question of that. His very name emulated the founding dynasty of this realm, thousands of years before the Blast, or so the local mythologies had it. No doubt Ch'in's public relations department had had a hand in that. But her studies had also pinpointed Ch'in for what he was: a pompous, arrogant, middle-aged prince with the supreme good fortune to have a loyal tactical genius for an adviser. Thus Ch'in could sate himself with ever-younger brides while his masterfully managed empire expanded. Many women were flattered to attract his roving eye and to join his luxurious harem; Soli was not. She had long since chosen her man, and she was not readily diverted.

But there remained the problem of foiling Ch'in while snaring Var. She had confidence in her ability to do either but not to do them simultaneously.

Var had come to her at last, barely before graduation —but, manlike, he had bungled it. He had tried to scale the wall and had been intercepted by Ch'in's minions and questioned and deported. She had asked the head matron to intercede, and that stern, kindly, courageous woman had obliged. So Var had been reprieved of his folly and set down in another territory, unharmed, with money. He would be safe for the time being, so long as he did nothing else foolish.

Still she slept fitfully. For the situation was by no means tied up neatly, and many things could go wrong. She had not yet decided how to deal with Ch'in. If she simply refused to oblige him, she might find herself kidnapped and ravished and murdered. The emperor had an infamous temper, especially when his pride was bruised. And the school would suffer too, perhaps harshly. No—an outright balk would not be expedient.

She could give Ch'in a gala wedding night, then spin a tearful tale of frustrated love. A proper appeal to his protective vanity might work wonders, particularly if the suggestion of political advantage were not too subtle. A romantically enhanced image would mitigate the effect of certain crude military policies, such as dethumbing valiant prisoners and selling them to gladiatorial arenas. Not that Ch'in was the only offender; the practice was general. But still it rankled. Image was very important here.

Yes, the wedding ploy seemed best. She could always run away after a reasonable interval if her plan didn't work. That way the school would not be blamed. Then she could locate Var and bring him to terms.

Except—she was not sure of Var. Oh, she could bring out the male in him, no question of that. But she distrusted his common sense. She could not assume that he would *not* do anything foolhardy. He might get tardily jealous and make some blundering move against Ch'in, or even come back to the school before graduation. Var just was not bright about such things, and he could be preposterously stubborn. His defiance of Minos had been incredible folly. . . .

And of course that was why she loved him.

Maybe she had been wrong to encourage him to seek the Chinese Helicon. There was one, somewhere, but they were obviously not at all close to it. Probably its underworlders were fully as secretive as those of the American unit, so that such a search would be quite difficult. But her purpose had not been to *find* it, only to give Var a suitable mission. A mission she could participate in, while she grew.

She wondered what had happened to her father and the Nameless One. Had they finally given up the chase? She doubted it. Once she had Var in hand, she would have to arrange a reconciliation. It had hurt her to run from Sol, but she knew she could not return to Helicon with him, and it was essential to keep track of Var. Sol had been the man of her childhood; Var was to be the man of her womanhood.

But the thought of Helicon reminded her of Sosa, the only mother she remembered. In certain ways the loss of Sosa was worse than that of Sol. What was that proud small woman doing now? Had she resigned herself to the absence of both husband and daughter? Soli doubted it, and this hurt.

Finally her memories and alarms and conjectures subsided, and she slept.

Ch'in was more portly than she had heard. In fact he was fat. His face retained the suggestion of lines that in youth would have been handsome, but he was long past youth. Not even the grandeur of his robes could render him esthetic.

Soli glimpsed him momentarily as she peered from a front window graduation morning. He was reviewing his troops, not even bothering to rise from the plush seat of his chauffeured open car. Suddenly she was unsure of her ability to play on his emotions; he looked too set, too jaded to be affected by a mere girl.

She ate a swift breakfast and performed her toilette: first a warm shower, then a tediously meticulous dressing, layer by layer. Then the combing of her hair to make it lustrous; nailfiling, makeup, a complete conversion process, to convert girl into lady. She inspected herself thoroughly in the mirror.

She was a colorful creature of skirts and frills and beads and sparkles. Her feet appeared tiny in the artful slippers, her face elfin under the spreading hat. No woman in America wore clothing like this, yet it was not unattractive.

The graduation ceremony occurred precisely on schedule. Thirty-five girls received their diplomas and minced single file to the courtyard where proud relatives awaited them. Soli was last, a place of honor, for it was acknowledgment that small attention would accrue to any girl following her. This was partly because she was the lone representative of her race. But she was also aware that though she was younger than some—thirteen—she was beautiful in her own right. She knew this because it was to her advantage to know it, and she possessed the poise to show herself off properly. Had she not mastered the essential techniques, she would not have graduated.

Ch'in was waiting for her buttressed by a phalanx of soldiers. He was resplendent in a semi-military uniform girt with medals and sashes; indeed, had he been smaller around the middle there might not have been room for all the decorations. But of course he wore no golden bracelet, and that made all the difference.

She smiled at him, turning her face to catch the sunlight momentarily so that her eyes and teeth flashed. Then she walked to him, moving her body with just that flair to heighten breast and hip and slender waist, and took his hands.

Oh, she was giving the audience the show Ch'in had bought. She *had* to sparkle, to validate the training she had had. Appearance was everything.

The emperor turned, and she turned with him as though connected and accompanied him toward the royal car.

People thronged behind the line of guards, eager for an envious glimpse of the Emperor and his lovely bride. Most were locals, owing no present allegiance to Ch'in but fascinated by the trappings of power—and well aware that tomorrow or next year they might very well come to owe him that allegiance. But a number had evidently traveled far for this occasion. Conspicuously absent were the patrols of the monarch of this territory; he wanted no trouble at all with Ch'in.

Near the polished car stood a somber, cloaked man. Momentarily she met his gaze, glanced on—

"Sol!" she whispered.

The sight of her father, so unexpected after five years and thousands of miles, overwhelmed her. She had seen him last in Helicon, but his dear face was still as familiar to her as any she knew.

Ch'in heard her exclamation and followed her gaze. "Who is that man?" he demanded.

The soldiers whirled immediately and grasped Sol. His hands came into sight and she saw that his left thumb was gone.

First she felt shock, then fury. *They had sold her father as a gladiator!* And, unreasonably, she fixed the blame on Ch'in.

She struck, using the technique Sosa had versed her in so well. Ch'in gasped and tottered, completely surprised. The soldiers drew their pistols.

Then Sol was moving, striking left and right, throwing the guards aside. A sword appeared in his hand. He leaped and came to stand beside Soli, the blade at Ch'in's throat.

The cordon of soldiers broke, letting the amazed spectators throng close. Soli saw guns level and knew that Sol would be killed where he stood whatever he did. There were too many troops, too many guns. Someone would shoot in the confusion, even though it cost the life of the emperor.

Then grotesque figures rose up within the crowd and began throwing people about. Gladiators—rampaging outside their arena! Hungry tigers could not have wreaked more havoc! In moments, every man with a gun had been incapacitated. Some weapons were fired, but not with accuracy. The melee became inchoate and purely muscular.

Sol pushed Ch'in roughly away, put his arm about Soli and lifted her into the car. A giant hurled the chauffeur out and vaulted into the driver's seat. The motor roared. Two more tremendous men piled on, shaking the vehicle as it moved out. They held curved bright swords aloft and swung them warningly at other trespassers. When the car became mired in the press of surrounding bodies these two jumped down to shove people out of the way of the wheels, working so quickly that no organized resistance could develop.

Soli hung on and watched. Suddenly she recognized the driver. He was the Nameless One, the man who had sworn to kill Var!

Now there were shots and screams, as the departure of the gladiators allowed the soldiers to recover their guns. But the crowd was such that the bullets scored only on innocent targets, not the fugitives. Then the car was finally free of the press and speeding over the roadway. Soli had supposed the vehicle was just for show, but it was a fully functioning machine.

"Hope Var makes it," the Nameless One said, glancing back.

"Var?" she asked breathlessly. "You found Var?"

"He found us. Freed us. Brought us here. We were—" He held up the stub of his thumb.

"You didn't fight? You and Var?" But obviously they hadn't.

"Do you want to travel with the wild boy?" he asked instead.

She wondered why the Nameless One should care how she felt about Var. But she answered. "Yes."

The car sped on, northward.

CHAPTER 20

Var, galvanized into action when he heard the shots, started the truck and nudged forward toward the crowd. If Soli had been hurt, he would run down the emperor!

Then he saw the car pull out, the Master driving, Soli beside him, two gladiators aboard. They had done it!

But the troops, only temporarily nonplussed, were massing, leveling their rifles. Var goosed the motor and careened across their path, spoiling their aim while the car fled. Men jumped at him. He veered, then recognized the naked thews of the remaining two gladiators. He eased up, allowing them to clamber aboard. Then he took off.

No one else got hold of the truck, not with those two free-swinging bodyguards on it. But there were no other vehicles to cross his own path and interfere with the aim of those rifles. There were shots; his tires popped. Var drove doggedly on, knowing that if he stopped for anything they all were doomed.

The wheel wrenched at his hand. The motor slowed and knocked. He used the clutch, raced the engine, and eased it back into harness. The truck bobbled and throbbed with the irregularity of skewed rubber, but it moved.

It was not fast enough. The troops had been left behind, and now a hillock in the road cut off the direct fire, but other cars would catch up in minutes. "We'll have to run for it!" Var cried as the motor finally overheated and stalled.

They piled out and charged into the forest as the first pursuing car appeared. There were cries and shots as the troops spied the truck, not realizing that it was empty.

Var and the two gladiators kept running, knowing the emperor's men would pick up their trail soon enough. Alone, he could have lost himself easily, for the forest was his natural habitat and he could hide in the badlands. But the other men, skilled as they might be in combat, were behemoths here. The end was inevitable unless they separated soon.

He could elude the gladiators. No problem about that. But was it fair? They had helped him free Soli, at the risk of their lives, and one of them was wounded in that action. Though he had freed *them* initially, at the risk of his own welfare. Where did the onus lie?"

"We have repaid you," one of the men panted. "Now we must hide among our own people, as you cannot. Otherwise we all will die, for Ch'in is ruthless."

"Yes," Var agreed. "You owe me nothing. It is fair."

The gladiator nodded. "It is fair. We regret, but it must be."

They thought they were protecting *him!* And that he would die if they deserted him. The three had almost brought destruction on their own heads through misplaced loyalty.

"It is fair. Go your way," Var repeated. He saluted them both and faded into the wilderness.

Secure at last from pursuit, he had opportunity to worry about the others. Soli and her father and the Master had driven north. Would they be able to outdistance the emperor's men and make a lasting escape? And if they did, could he locate them?

In fact, would they let him locate them? Sol had been reunited with his daughter, after Var had inadvertently kept them apart these long years. They could go home to America. They did not need the wild boy. And might not *want* him. For what would he do, except try to take Soli away again?

If Soli had any such inclination. Now he doubted it. She had been furious when he put her in the school, and cool to him since the few times he had seen her at all privately. She had been set up for an excellent marriage until he had arranged to break it up. Now she was with her father, a better man than Var. Surely she would either stay with Sol or go back to Emperor Ch'in.

So he would be best advised to hide in the badlands and let her go her way.

He circled back to the road, knowing no one would expect to find him there, and trotted in the direction the car had gone, north. He never *had* taken the best advice.

Every so often a vehicle passed, and Var leaped into the ditch and hid, emerging immediately afterwards to continue his solitary trek. Sooner or later he would catch up to the car or discover the trail where the party left it. Then. . . .

Another truck was bouncing south, and he jumped for cover. He smelled the dust of it, underlaid by gas fumes, manure odor . . . and Soli's perfume.

He charged into the road, shouting. Either Ch'in's men had captured her already, or—

The truck stopped. Soli stepped down prettily and waved her bonnet, looking incredibly genteel. "Get in, you idiot!" she cried. "I knew you'd get lost."

So the four were together for the first time: Var, Soli, Sol and the Master. The two remaining gladiators had gone their own ways, having fulfilled their obligation.

"Now we'll have to plan our escape," the Master said as he drove. "There'll be roadblocks. We fooled them by doubling back in another vehicle, but that won't work a second time. So we'll have to take to the hills soon, and they'll be tracking us with dogs. This Ch'in is not one to give up readily, and that general of his is an expert at this sort of chase. We'll probably take losses, better count on fifty percent."

Var didn't recognize the term. "How many?"

"Two of us may die."

Var looked at Soli. She perched on Sol's lap between Var and the Master, and her elegant coiffure was undisturbed. She was as lovely and distant a lady as he had ever seen, and a striking contrast to the brutish, stinking men about her. How well she had responded to the training!

And how aloof from him now! His tentative fancies were ludicrous. She had no need of him. She was with her father again, and the chase was over, and Var was superfluous. They had returned to pick him up out of common courtesy, no more.

"You've been here a year, Var," the Master said. "You know the region. What's our best escape route, and where can we make a stand if caught?"

Var pondered it. "The land is fairly open to the south, but that's Ch'in's territory. There are mountain ranges east and west, so that no truck roads go through, though we could

scale one of the passes on foot. Except for the dogs," he
added, realizing that they *had* to stay with the vehicle. "To
the north is really best, except for the—"

He stopped, appreciating as he suspected the Master had
already, the predicament they were in. Far north the land
was wild and open, so that pursuit would be awkward even
with many men and dogs. Wild tribes fought anything resembling an organized, civilized force, but tended to ignore
refugees. Ideal for this group. But the near north was a
bottleneck. Hardly fifty miles beyond the area where he had
found the gladiators potent badlands began. These intense
bands of radiation extended east and west for hundreds of
miles, acting as an invulnerable natural barrior between the
civilized southerners and the primitive tribes.

Only one road went through, for only one pass was clear
of the deadly emanations, and that barely. This was fortified
and always garrisoned; he and Soli had had to pass through
it and pay token toll even as foot travelers on their original
journey south. This was not in Ch'in's domain, but the personnel were friendly to him. Ch'in's public relations with
such key outposts were uniformly good, one of the reasons
his power was on the ascent.

"I think we shall have to take the badlands pass," the
Master said.

No one answered. The feat was of course impossible.

"In my time as a gladiator," the Master said, "I pondered
this as a theoretical problem. How half a dozen bold men
might overcome the garrison and hold the pass indefinitely."

"But we are four!" Var protested, knowing that with
even a hundred it could not be done. That fortress had
balked entire armies in the past.

The Nameless One shrugged and drove on. When they
passed other vehicles the passengers hunched down so as not
to attract unwelcome attention. In due course he turned off
the main road, heading toward the badlands section adjacent
to the pass. "Give warning," he said to Var.

Var gave warning. The Master stopped immediately and
backed away from the radiation thus advertised. "Now find a
hot rock that we can put aboard with some shielding.
Several, in fact. Don't touch them, of course, just point
them out. We'll rig a derrick and hook them in at the end
of a pole. A ten-foot pole," he said, smiling momentarily
for some reason.

It was done. Var located several small stones with intense radioactivity, and they maneuvered them into the back of the truck by rope and stick. The men were dosed, inevitably, but not seriously. Soli looked on, concerned and not quite approving. Var privately agreed with her. This was dangerous work, to no apparent purpose, and it consumed time far better spent in fleeing the searching Ch'in forces.

Then they dumped larger rocks and dirt into the main body of the truck, to serve as a shield between the cab and the radiation. When Var pronounced the cab clean, they poured their remaining fuel—the last of several big cans the truck carried as a standard precaution, since fuel stations were far between—into the tank and set off for the pass.

"Now comes the rough part," the Master said as they ground up the winding approach. "The garrison had geiger counters, and we can be sure they're thoroughly leery of radiation. In fact, this is known as a hardship post, because of that danger. There's a rapid turnover in personnel, to prevent low-grade illness from peripheral radiation, too."

The Master had obviously done more than just think about that pass. He had studied it, probably reading books on the subject. Var wondered how a gladiator would get hold of books. But no amount of study could get them past.

"Those men will shy away from radiation automatically, and go into blind terror if trapped in it," the Master said.

"Who wouldn't?" Soli inquired. "It's a horrible death. I bit my tongue three times just watching you play with those stones."

Var remembered the Master's own experience with radiation in the American badlands and marveled that he was not more leery of it himself. But he was beginning to see some method in this cargo. They carried a truckload of terror. . . .

"We can use this to drive them off," the Master said. "They won't even shoot, because that could blast radioactive fragments all over the station. They'll retreat with alacrity. They'll have to."

"But why should they fear it in a shielded truck?" Var asked.

"It won't stay in the truck. We'll bring it inside."

Var felt a shock of horror he knew the others shared. "Carry it? Without the poles?"

"Two people can do the job. And hold the pass for hours

afterward. So two can escape and reach the wilds and later
the coast, and—"

"No!" Var and Soli cried together.

"I did mention fifty percent casualties," the Nameless One
replied. "Perhaps you youngsters have become softened by
civilized life. Have you any illusions what it would mean to
fall into the hands of Ch'in's men now? We shall surely do
so if we do not escape this region promptly. Already the dogs
must have been unleashed, and those hounds are not gentle
either. Sol and I have met a few in our business."

Var knew he was right. The gladiators were better equipped
to face reality and to take the prospect of torture and
death in stride. They had to get through the pass, and they
could not do so by bluff. They were known now, and their
crime was known, and these soldiers were tough and disciplined. No appeal would move them, no ruse confound
them, no empty threat cow them. Nothing short of artillery
would dislodge them . . . except radiation.

"Who escapes?" Soli asked in a small voice.

"You do," the Master said brusquely. "And one to guard
you."

"Who?" Soli asked again.

"One close to you. One you trust. One you love." A pause,
then: "Not me."

That left two to choose from, Var saw. Himself and Sol.
He understood what was necessary. "Her father."

"Sol," the Master said quickly.

Sol, being voiceless, did not say anything.

So it was decided. Var felt cold all through, knowing he
was going to die, and not swiftly. His skin would warn him
of radiation, but could not protect him otherwise. He survived it by avoiding it, where others received fatal dosages
unawares. If he touched one of those stones . . .

Yet there was a morbid satisfaction in it too. He had
never asked for more than the right to live and die beside
the Master. Now he would do so. Soli would be saved and
her father would guard her, as he had before. They would
return to America, to the land of true solace, land of the
circle code. He felt a tremendous nostalgia for it, for its
courtesies and combats, even for the crazy crazies.

That was what meant most to Var: that Soli be safe and
happy and home. That was what he had really tried, so un-
successfully, to arrange for her before. A safe, happy home.

He would die thinking of her, loving her.

The challenge point came into sight. Metal bars closed off the road. As the truck stopped before them, other bars dropped behind, powered by a massive winch. "Dismount!" the guard bellowed from his interior tower.

The four got down and lined up before the truck.

"That's the girl!" the guard cried. "Ch'in's bride, the foreign piece!"

The Master turned, and suddenly a bow was in his hands, an arrow nocked, loosed, swishing up—and the tower guard collapsed silently, the missile through his windpipe.

Now was the time to pick up the rocks. Var stepped toward the back, girding himself for the flashing pain of contact, and the Master's huge hand fell on his arm. Var stumbled back, bewildered. Then he was shoved brusquely forward.

At the same time Sol whirled on his daughter, grasping her by the upper arms and lifting her bodily before him. She and Var met face to face, involuntarily, each held from behind. The Master's hand clapped down on Var's wrist, twisting off the bracelet. Sol reached out to take it and shove it onto Soli's wrist and squeeze it tight. Then Var and Soli were dropped, clutching at each other to keep from falling.

As they disengaged and righted themselves, they saw that Sol and the Nameless One had already grabbed hot stones. The two men leaped for either side of the grating, climbing rapidly with the deadly stones tucked into their waistbands. That was a talent the Master had not had before! They were at the top by the time the other guards discovered what had happened.

The Master hurled a stone toward a panel. "Listen!" he bellowed. Var heard the fevered chatter of crazy-type click-boxes, the screams of amazement and fear.

The Master began to crank up the forward grill. Var saw the counterweights descending, the road opening ahead.

"Drive!" the Master shouted down. Var obeyed unthinkingly. He scrambled into the driver's seat, Soli into the other. The motor was running; it had never been turned off, he realized only now. The Master had planned every detail.

As the gate cleared, he nudged out. The top of the cab scraped the bars; then they were free.

As he started down the north slope, Var heard the portcullis crash behind. The Master had let it drop suddenly. Probably he had cut the counterweight rope, so that the barrier could not be lifted again without tedious repairs. There would be no vehicle pursuit.

Safely away from the fortress, Var braked the truck. "This isn't right," he said, recovering equillibrium. "*I* should be back there."

"No," Soli said. "This is the way they meant it to be."

"But Soli—"

"Vara," she said.

Var stared at the gold band on her wrist, realizing what it meant. "But did I. . . ?"

"Yes, you did," she said.

Var was silent for a long time. At last he was seeing things clearly.

"We must go back to America and tell them what we know: that we have seen the rest of the world, that what we have at home is best, and we dare not destroy it through empire. Helicon must be rebuilt, the nomads must disband, the guns must be abolished. We shall go to the crazy demesnes and tell them."

"Yes, my husband," Vara said, admiring the new tone of power in Var's speech.

"For Sos and Sol sacrificed themselves for us, friends at the end. We must not allow America to be divided into war-ring camps."

He put his arm around Vara, his wife, his rugged companion. As the shadows lengthened before them, they sat facing the East, where their long journey would take them. Tomorrow they were starting home.